I0645170

CITY OF GHOSTS

(An Ava Gold Mystery—Book Four)

BLAKE PIERCE

Blake Pierce

Blake Pierce is the USA Today bestselling author of the RILEY PAGE mystery series, which includes seventeen books. Blake Pierce is also the author of the MACKENZIE WHITE mystery series, comprising fourteen books; of the AVERY BLACK mystery series, comprising six books; of the KERI LOCKE mystery series, comprising five books; of the MAKING OF RILEY PAIGE mystery series, comprising six books; of the KATE WISE mystery series, comprising seven books; of the CHLOE FINE psychological suspense mystery, comprising six books; of the JESSE HUNT psychological suspense thriller series, comprising twenty one books; of the AU PAIR psychological suspense thriller series, comprising three books; of the ZOE PRIME mystery series, comprising six books; of the ADELE SHARP mystery series, comprising fifteen books, of the EUROPEAN VOYAGE cozy mystery series, comprising four books; of the new LAURA FROST FBI suspense thriller, comprising six books (and counting); of the new ELLA DARK FBI suspense thriller, comprising eleven books (and counting); of the A YEAR IN EUROPE cozy mystery series, comprising nine books, of the AVA GOLD mystery series, comprising six books (and counting); and of the RACHEL GIFT mystery series, comprising six books (and counting).

An avid reader and lifelong fan of the mystery and thriller genres, Blake loves to hear from you, so please feel free to visit www.blakepierceauthor.com to learn more and stay in touch.

Copyright © 2022 by Blake Pierce. All rights reserved. Except as permitted under the U.S. Copyright Act of 1976, no part of this publication may be reproduced, distributed or transmitted in any form or by any means, or stored in a database or retrieval system, without the prior permission of the author. This ebook is licensed for your personal enjoyment only. This ebook may not be re-sold or given away to other people. If you would like to share this book with another person, please purchase an additional copy for each recipient. If you're reading this book and did not purchase it, or it was not purchased for your use only, then please return it and purchase your own copy. Thank you for respecting the hard work of this author. This is a work of fiction. Names, characters, businesses, organizations, places, events, and incidents either are the product of the author's imagination or are used fictionally. Any resemblance to actual persons, living or dead, is entirely coincidental. Jacket image Copyright Everett Collection used under license from Shutterstock.com.
ISBN: 978-1-0943-7629-5

BOOKS BY BLAKE PIERCE

RACHEL GIFT MYSTERY SERIES
HER LAST WISH (Book #1)
HER LAST CHANCE (Book #2)
HER LAST HOPE (Book #3)
HER LAST FEAR (Book #4)
HER LAST CHOICE (Book #5)
HER LAST BREATH (Book #6)

AVA GOLD MYSTERY SERIES
CITY OF PREY (Book #1)
CITY OF FEAR (Book #2)
CITY OF BONES (Book #3)
CITY OF GHOSTS (Book #4)
CITY OF DEATH (Book #5)
CITY OF VICE (Book #6)

A YEAR IN EUROPE
A MURDER IN PARIS (Book #1)
DEATH IN FLORENCE (Book #2)
VENGEANCE IN VIENNA (Book #3)
A FATALITY IN SPAIN (Book #4)

ELLA DARK FBI SUSPENSE THRILLER
GIRL, ALONE (Book #1)
GIRL, TAKEN (Book #2)
GIRL, HUNTED (Book #3)
GIRL, SILENCED (Book #4)
GIRL, VANISHED (Book 5)
GIRL ERASED (Book #6)
GIRL, FORSAKEN (Book #7)
GIRL, TRAPPED (Book #8)
GIRL, EXPENDABLE (Book #9)
GIRL, ESCAPED (Book #10)
GIRL, HIS (Book #11)

LAURA FROST FBI SUSPENSE THRILLER

ALREADY GONE (Book #1)
ALREADY SEEN (Book #2)
ALREADY TRAPPED (Book #3)
ALREADY MISSING (Book #4)
ALREADY DEAD (Book #5)
ALREADY TAKEN (Book #6)

EUROPEAN VOYAGE COZY MYSTERY SERIES
MURDER (AND BAKLAVA) (Book #1)
DEATH (AND APPLE STRUDEL) (Book #2)
CRIME (AND LAGER) (Book #3)
MISFORTUNE (AND GOUDA) (Book #4)
CALAMITY (AND A DANISH) (Book #5)
MAYHEM (AND HERRING) (Book #6)

ADELE SHARP MYSTERY SERIES
LEFT TO DIE (Book #1)
LEFT TO RUN (Book #2)
LEFT TO HIDE (Book #3)
LEFT TO KILL (Book #4)
LEFT TO MURDER (Book #5)
LEFT TO ENVY (Book #6)
LEFT TO LAPSE (Book #7)
LEFT TO VANISH (Book #8)
LEFT TO HUNT (Book #9)
LEFT TO FEAR (Book #10)
LEFT TO PREY (Book #11)
LEFT TO LURE (Book #12)
LEFT TO CRAVE (Book #13)
LEFT TO LOATHE (Book #14)
LEFT TO HARM (Book #15)

THE AU PAIR SERIES
ALMOST GONE (Book#1)
ALMOST LOST (Book #2)
ALMOST DEAD (Book #3)

ZOE PRIME MYSTERY SERIES
FACE OF DEATH (Book#1)
FACE OF MURDER (Book #2)

FACE OF FEAR (Book #3)
FACE OF MADNESS (Book #4)
FACE OF FURY (Book #5)
FACE OF DARKNESS (Book #6)

A JESSIE HUNT PSYCHOLOGICAL SUSPENSE SERIES
THE PERFECT WIFE (Book #1)
THE PERFECT BLOCK (Book #2)
THE PERFECT HOUSE (Book #3)
THE PERFECT SMILE (Book #4)
THE PERFECT LIE (Book #5)
THE PERFECT LOOK (Book #6)
THE PERFECT AFFAIR (Book #7)
THE PERFECT ALIBI (Book #8)
THE PERFECT NEIGHBOR (Book #9)
THE PERFECT DISGUISE (Book #10)
THE PERFECT SECRET (Book #11)
THE PERFECT FAÇADE (Book #12)
THE PERFECT IMPRESSION (Book #13)
THE PERFECT DECEIT (Book #14)
THE PERFECT MISTRESS (Book #15)
THE PERFECT IMAGE (Book #16)
THE PERFECT VEIL (Book #17)
THE PERFECT INDISCRETION (Book #18)
THE PERFECT RUMOR (Book #19)
THE PERFECT COUPLE (Book #20)
THE PERFECT MURDER (Book #21)

CHLOE FINE PSYCHOLOGICAL SUSPENSE SERIES
NEXT DOOR (Book #1)
A NEIGHBOR'S LIE (Book #2)
CUL DE SAC (Book #3)
SILENT NEIGHBOR (Book #4)
HOMECOMING (Book #5)
TINTED WINDOWS (Book #6)

KATE WISE MYSTERY SERIES
IF SHE KNEW (Book #1)
IF SHE SAW (Book #2)
IF SHE RAN (Book #3)

IF SHE HID (Book #4)
IF SHE FLED (Book #5)
IF SHE FEARED (Book #6)
IF SHE HEARD (Book #7)

THE MAKING OF RILEY PAIGE SERIES
WATCHING (Book #1)
WAITING (Book #2)
LURING (Book #3)
TAKING (Book #4)
STALKING (Book #5)
KILLING (Book #6)

RILEY PAIGE MYSTERY SERIES
ONCE GONE (Book #1)
ONCE TAKEN (Book #2)
ONCE CRAVED (Book #3)
ONCE LURED (Book #4)
ONCE HUNTED (Book #5)
ONCE PINED (Book #6)
ONCE FORSAKEN (Book #7)
ONCE COLD (Book #8)
ONCE STALKED (Book #9)
ONCE LOST (Book #10)
ONCE BURIED (Book #11)
ONCE BOUND (Book #12)
ONCE TRAPPED (Book #13)
ONCE DORMANT (Book #14)
ONCE SHUNNED (Book #15)
ONCE MISSED (Book #16)
ONCE CHOSEN (Book #17)

MACKENZIE WHITE MYSTERY SERIES
BEFORE HE KILLS (Book #1)
BEFORE HE SEES (Book #2)
BEFORE HE COVETS (Book #3)
BEFORE HE TAKES (Book #4)
BEFORE HE NEEDS (Book #5)
BEFORE HE FEELS (Book #6)
BEFORE HE SINS (Book #7)

BEFORE HE HUNTS (Book #8)
BEFORE HE PREYS (Book #9)
BEFORE HE LONGS (Book #10)
BEFORE HE LAPSES (Book #11)
BEFORE HE ENVIES (Book #12)
BEFORE HE STALKS (Book #13)
BEFORE HE HARMS (Book #14)

AVERY BLACK MYSTERY SERIES
CAUSE TO KILL (Book #1)
CAUSE TO RUN (Book #2)
CAUSE TO HIDE (Book #3)
CAUSE TO FEAR (Book #4)
CAUSE TO SAVE (Book #5)
CAUSE TO DREAD (Book #6)

KERI LOCKE MYSTERY SERIES
A TRACE OF DEATH (Book #1)
A TRACE OF MURDER (Book #2)
A TRACE OF VICE (Book #3)
A TRACE OF CRIME (Book #4)
A TRACE OF HOPE (Book #5)

CHAPTER ONE

It was another of those days where Eve felt like a rat rather than a woman. As she worked her way through the crowded apartment building with a wet basket of the day's laundry, she thought of the rats she'd sometimes seen back in Poland, racing through the streets after a heavy rain to keep from drowning. Eve had come to New York two months ago with hardly any money in her pocket—money that was essentially meaningless in this hardened American city. She'd discovered quite quickly that the vast majority of the poor immigrants were finding shelter on the Lower East side, where land and apartments were cheap.

But her apartment, which she shared with two other single women and two entire families, was starting to feel more like a zoo than a home. She worked her way through the small den where three of the seven children from the two families were currently playing a very disorganized game of jacks. The father of the most recent addition, a thin rail of a man that was constantly smoking cheap, hand rolled cigarettes, sat in the corner on a striped cushion. His eyes devoured Eve's fit, twenty-four-year-old frame as she passed by.

When she stepped out of the side door, away from his gaze and the children's noise, she felt as if she'd stepped into the most refreshing water imaginable. That was saying something, too; the alleyway between their apartment building and the neighboring building was filthy. Garbage from the tenants in both buildings was stacked against the walls, refuse spilling everywhere. As Eve stepped out to one of the meager little clotheslines that was strung between the two buildings, she watched as two stray dogs began tearing into one of the bags. The alley, thin and decrepit as it was, always seemed to be alive with some form of activity or another. In the short two months that she'd been here, Eve had seen two brawls between drunken men and had even stepped outside early one morning to a pair of poor, starved lovers making love against the side of the neighboring wall.

This morning, closing in on the afternoon, the dogs and Eve were the only inhabitants of the urine-scented alley, though. She could hear the city, busy and alive, through the cramped space of the alley and she wondered if her life would ever change here. She'd already inquired about a potential job as a seamstress's assistant and her father started his job as a dockworker in a few days. But in a city of this size where immigrants were hated more and more every day, it was hard to imagine any sort of real change occurring anytime soon.

As she strung the hand-washed laundry from the clothesline, one of the children inside cheered loudly, apparently coming out victorious. Before coming to New York, Eve had always assumed she'd have children—at least three of them. Of course, a husband needed to come first. And while Eve knew she was considered something of a treat for the eyes, she also knew that no self-respecting man in this city would consider a life with a poor immigrant—not outside of a single night of drunken bliss. She'd heard of some women offering themselves for a night or two out near the docks, just as a way to make some money and get a head start on a so-called better life. But Eve would not subject herself to such humiliation. She'd only ever been with one man, and he had died just a few weeks before her ship had left to bring her to this city. She didn't intend to be intimate with another man until she was properly wed.

The laugh that came from her mouth at this thought was a sad sound indeed. Here she was, thinking about marriage when she didn't even know where her next meal was coming from. She was quite certain there were a few slices of cheese left, and her father had managed to bring some bread home yesterday. She supposed if they—

She heard a slight movement from ahead of her. She couldn't see what it was because she'd just hung one of her father's larger work shirts on the line. She guessed it was one of the kids from inside, maybe coming out for some fresh air or to throw things at the stray dogs. Or, worse yet, it could be their father, coming out to leer at her a bit more and with more fire while his children were not there to witness it.

Cringing, she dared a glance around the hanging, wet shirt. One of her tops was in her other hand and as she stretched it out to hang over the line, she also peered around her father's shirt.

There *was* a man there, but it was not the perverted father from inside. In fact, Eve had never seen this face. It was not one of the tenants from her apartment and she was pretty sure it was no one from the neighboring building.

"Yes?" she asked.

Already, she was scared. There was something in this man's eyes that unsettled her, a dark sort of burning that made her think her goal of keeping herself pure until she was wed again may be foolish. This man had the look of someone that was going to take what he wanted even if—

He moved with incredibly speed. He had something in his hand, a piece of clothing that, in a silly final thought, she assumed he wanted to hang from the clothesline. Was it a scarf? Maybe a handkerchief of some kind?

Eve didn't know. What she *did* know was that he had no intention of hanging it. Instead, he came forward, brushing past her father's wet shirt, and swooped the piece of clothing around her neck. Before she could cry out in fear and confusion, she felt a hard elbow go right into her ribs. Something pinched and broke, and as she sucked in a hiss of pain, she realized that her throat was closed off.

The man pulled tightly to the fabric around her neck, so hard and tight that she could feel the cloth trying to cut into the flesh of her neck. She struggled as he pulled even tighter and pushed her against the wall. Her vision grew blurry, but she could still see him as he pressed her against the wall and stared into her eyes. She closed her own eyes, knowing that she was going to die and not wanting to see that absolute fury and fire in the man's eyes.

Her lungs screamed for air but there was none to be had. She felt her body giving away, her knees sagging, and she once again thought of those rats back at home, running so hard and with such desperation even though something in their very posture seemed to know that there was no use—that the water would catch up and the end would wash over them no matter what they did.

CHAPTER TWO

Ava Gold watched the two men just outside of the tobacco shop, hoping one of them would do something even the least bit incriminating so she'd have an excuse to arrest one of them. To anyone else, she assumed they both looked prim and proper, respectable gentlemen that had just come from inside the tobacco shop after purchasing some cigars. They were dressed in nice, thin coats and both wore brimmed hats. There appeared to be nothing amiss about them.

But Ava was quite sure one of them—the shorter, slightly cherubic one—had killed her husband. She'd recently learned through records and old paperwork that his name was Jim Spurlock. Though he had only a few minor dings on his record, Ava was starting to suspect he may be one of those criminals that was heavily involved in just about everything but was slippery enough to never get caught.

Ava was currently leaning against the wall of the butcher shop on the opposite side of the street. She was pretending to read the newspaper, where a few different stories told the same tale about a deteriorating financial sector—all news that Ava honestly couldn't care less about. She held the paper in front of her face and watched the two men. She'd been trailing Spurlock for three days now, just waiting for him to mess up *just enough.*

But so far, there had been nothing. If anything, tailing Spurlock had helped her to understand that as September slowly came to an end, she had somehow started to live what felt like three different lives. She loved each of those lives but balancing them was starting to become very difficult.

The first life was perhaps her favorite; it was the life where she had a living son and a protective father. They all lived together and here, nearly four months after Clarence had died, she was just now starting to get her feet under her. She was starting to feel like an adequate mother again, that the world was still full of possibilities for her son.

The second and third lives ran together, and the waters were often muddied. The second was centered around her new career as a successful and mostly respected detective with the NYPD. She'd been closing cases and proving herself more consistently than anyone could have expected. And as an offshoot of that second life, her third one stepped in. it came in the form of a secret hunt to find her husband's killer. The NYPD had been perfectly fine chalking it up to "murderer escaped, never seen again." That was the exact verbiage in Clarence Gold's case file. But Ava Gold was not about to rest easy with that explanation. Not when some simple research and hard work had led her here—to eyeing a man she was quite certain was her husband's killer from across the street.

As the men finally move away from the shop, Ava folded her paper and, after giving them some space, she followed along behind them. It was nearing the end of the workday and these two seemed to be in a good mood. She had no idea what Jim Spurlock did for a living. For all she knew, he was one of those powerful stockbrokers or maybe he was connected to the mob and had a steady flow of money coming to him through several nefarious avenues.

All she really knew about him was that his description was on a few different records back at the police department. And when he was mentioned, some basic connect-the-dots to other cases usually lined him up fairly square. It wasn't because of any department negligence. Unless someone was actively trying to find dirt on the man, the search for such connections would have been quite exhaustive.

Jim Spurlock may have been short in stature, but it did not seem to bother him at all. He was nearly a whole foot shorter than the man he was walking beside but he carried himself with swagger and confidence. Yet, because of what Ava suspected the man to be guilty of, she'd started to think of him as a repugnant little troll.

She followed them for two more blocks before the taller man said his goodbyes and veered off, heading down 51st Street while Spurlock continued heading straight. It took a great deal of restraint for Ava to stay back. She would have loved nothing more than to rush up to the little troll, slam him against the wall and tell him she knew what he had done—that he'd killed her husband during a botched bank robbery, and probably several others over the past few years. But with a few months of basic training and detective intuition driving her, she knew this would do more harm than good. First of all, she wasn't entirely certain Spurlock was her husband's killer, though the physical description and the man's scattered criminal history backed up the suspicion. Secondly, if he *was* guilty, such treatment without any real reason would work to his favor when the case was taken to trial.

In other words, she knew the only way to nail him was to catch him doing something illegal and then connect the dots while he was in custody. And that was precisely why she'd been tailing him every chance she got. She now knew his daily routine, so finding him was never much of a problem; the problem came down to doing it in a way where Captain Minard or Frank would never know what she was doing.

Ah, hell…Frank, she thought.

She looked at her watch and saw that their dinner date was in an hour and a half. She still had a bit of time to follow after Spurlock, but not much. Tonight was a pretty big one. Frank was coming to her apartment to meet her father and Jeffrey. Frank had met her father briefly on one occasion, but they'd barely spoken. Tonight would make it official and if Ava was being honest with herself, she was quite nervous about it. She couldn't help but wonder if that was why she'd chosen to end her day tailing Spurlock; it was keeping her mind off of the heavy moment coming up later tonight.

She followed behind him, keeping about a half-block of space between them, for another ten minutes. He was heading to the Upper West Side, finally coming to a stop at the front of a plain-looking apartment building. There, he walked up the stairs and met with a woman standing by the door. They chatted in an animated fashion for bit, the woman pointing to a watch on her thin wrist several times.

After roughly a minute, Spurlock took the woman by the hand, and her posture relaxed. She then started to giggle and opened the door. When Spurlock followed her inside, still holding the woman's hand, he took a final look back onto the street as if making sure no one was watching him as he entered. His eyes never lingered on Ava, though she still worried that he'd spot her. Even if he did, though, he doubted he'd know who she was. While her name was rather common in the papers and she was gaining more and more attention with every cracked case, not many people knew her face.

The door to the building closed behind them and as Ava walked past it, she took note of the address. She committed it to memory, intending to add it to the growing pile of notes she had back at the station regarding Clarence's murder. She then came to the end of the block, crossed over, and headed back the way she'd come. Even after getting up from reading her newspaper, she'd followed Spurlock for eight blocks, and that was *after* already having followed him five blocks to the tobacco shop.

But she was fine with the walk. It gave her more time to prepare herself for her dinner with Frank and her family. She hated that she was so nervous about it. After all that she'd been through since Clarence's murder, why was something this trivial gnawing at her?

Deep down, she thought she knew why…but she wasn't ready to face it just yet. What she did know and could not escape, though, was that thinking of trying to bring Clarence's killer to justice while thinking of a dinner date with another man was its own special sort of emotional torture. And here she was, about to willingly step right into it.

CHAPTER THREE

She was shocked to find that both her father and Jeffrey had already started preparing dinner. Her father had never minded getting behind the stove and lending a hand when it was absolutely necessary, but she'd never seen this sort of initiative before. He'd started making the mix for cornbread and Jeffrey was busy carefully cutting up tomatoes. They both smiled at her when she entered, and she soaked the moment in. This was not only "her men" making sure dinner was ready, but it was also them letting her know that they were both okay with another man coming into their home—the first since Clarence had been taken from her.

"I don't know if you remember or not," Roosevelt said, "but my cornbread is legendary."

"I do," Ava said, washing her hands in the sink to join in as quickly as possible. "You going to give it that spice and kick I remember so well?"

"Of course."

"And the 'maters are for the biscuits we're going to make," Jeffrey added.

Ava did her best not to burst out into laughter at the way he said tomatoes. For some reason, it was a word he'd never properly mastered and her father had only encouraged it by mimicking the way the word was pronounced in the deep south to help him learn the word. She slid into the dinner-process naturally and within half an hour, the place was smelling of cornbread, biscuits, gravy, and sausage.

The biscuits weren't quite done when there was a knock at the door. Ava walked over to answer it but was instantly cut off by Jeffrey. He answered the door quickly, surprising Ava. She'd truly expected him to be unhappy about her courting another man—if that was indeed what she and Frank were doing. He even beat her to saying the first *hello*.

"Hi!" Jeffrey said, beaming up at Frank. "I'm Jeffrey!"

Frank seemed just as shocked as Ava felt, but he masked it quickly. He extended his hand to the boy and said, "Good to meet you, Jeffrey. I'm Frank. And you know…your mother talks about you a lot."

"She does?"

"Oh, for sure." He then looked up to Ava and cocked his head. "You look different when you're not at work."

"Is that good or bad?"

He smiled and said, "Oh, it's much better."

She turned away quickly, feeling herself start to blush. "Come on in."

Frank stepped inside, instantly removing the cap from his head. He tucked it under his arm and made a point to head directly over to her father. "Mr. Burr, it's so great to see you again." Again, he extended his hand, this time with a bit more authority than he had when he'd offered it to Jeffrey.

Roosevelt wiped his hands on the dish cloth he was holding and accepted. "Likewise," Roosevelt said.

"Anything I can do to help?" Frank asked.

"Just be patient and wait for these biscuits to come out."

"Yeah, our dinners are pretty basic," Ava said. "Sorry if you were expecting something a little more traditional."

"Um, excuse me," Roosevelt said. "Was that a slight against my cornbread?"

"Oh, I'm not a picky eater. You should know this by now. And besides, it smells amazing."

It took another five minutes for the biscuits to come out and when they did, they were piping hot. Frank insisted on slicing the cheese that Roosevelt took out if the icebox and together, they sat down to a dinner of sausage, cheese, and tomato biscuits. When Frank slid his through Roosevelt's thick gravy, she did not think he was simply playing a part when he insisted how delicious it was. She could see the truth of it in his eyes. It was an unexpected reminder of just how well she was getting to know him—able to read his non-verbal cues and know what he was thinking when words weren't used.

Conversation was mostly natural, spurred on by Jeffrey asking question about what his mother was like as a detective. Then, as Ava had pretty much expected, things turned to boxing. She was just surprised that it was Frank that brought it up rather than her father.

"So I need to get this out," Frank said. "Mr. Burr, I saw you fight twice when I was a teenager. My father was a huge fan."

"Did you get to see me win?"

"Once. The second time, you dropped the belt."

Roosevelt frowned playfully. "To Rusty Mulligan, right?"

"Yeah. It was a good fight, though."

"I guess. Now, you said your father was a big fan. What about you?"

It was Frank's turn to frown now. He looked to his biscuit guiltily for a moment before finally answering. "Bulldog Brody."

"Hey, nothing wrong with that! He was lightning fast! And my God, the left hook that kid had. Of course, he never beat me, so I can say all those nice things about him."

"Wait, did you ever fight him?"

"Twice! They fed him to me when he needed the experience coming up and then about a year later. He took me to five rounds, but I won with a knockout."

"Wow! I had no idea."

"Yeah!" Jeffrey beamed. "Grandpa didn't lose a lot. What about you, Detective Wimbly? Did you ever box?"

"No. But I do get into some fisticuffs with my job from time to time." He smiled and looked over to Ava before adding, "And so does your mom."

Jeffrey knew this but looked amazed all the same. Roosevelt looked at her proudly, munching on his cornbread. "You seen her right-handed jab?"

"Oh yeah," Frank said. "A few times."

It all went much smoother than Ava expected. She watched Frank interact with her family and was amazed at how natural it came to him. But as she felt this creating a warmth and security within her, she also felt a huge degree of guilt. She was growing very fond of him, but Clarence had not been gone six months yet. It felt too soon but, at the same time, it felt right. So what the hell was she supposed to do?

The conversation went from boxing and then to the weather, and then to the recent stories in the papers about growing restlessness on Wall Street.

"Bunch of rich men that never worked a day in their life, got no idea what to do with their money," Roosevelt said. "It's as simple as that."

"I agree with some of that," Ava said. "But we can't just dismiss it so easily. Some are saying if a blow comes to Wall Street, *all* of us will feel it."

"Now that doesn't seem quite fair, does it?" Roosevelt said.

"Sure doesn't," Frank agreed.

They left it at that, and Ava couldn't help but feel that it was because there was some truth to what she'd said. After all, they lived in New York City and though she and her father were currently doing okay for themselves, it would just take two or three bad months for them to start struggling. Maybe a blow to Wall Street and the way money moved through the city would impact them more than any of them realized. It almost seemed like an invitation to bad luck to even discuss it—and it was a very real feeling that permeated the dinner table.

The topic seemed to dampen the mood, though no one mentioned it. After the meal, they all cleaned up together and as Ava watched both her father and Frank help with the dishes, she understood just how fortunate she was. She knew not many men would volunteer to take on such duties, and the fact that her son was seeing the example did her heart good.

After dinner, Ava had expected a very awkward moment where the undecided nature of the rest of the night would go. Did she invite him to stay longer and have more conversation in the living room before Jeffrey went to bed? Did she treat it like an actual date and have him stay even longer? Well, that last option as basically out, as her father slept on the couch. But to her surprise, Frank made the entire ordeal easy for her.

As they finished the dishes, Jeffrey wiping down the table and her father wiping down the frying pan, Frank approached her from behind. He gently brushed her hand with his, though he did not take it, and said: "You want to walk me out?"

"Yeah, sure."

"Aww, you're leaving?" Jeffrey asked.

"Yeah, I sort of need to. It was a long day today and tomorrow is shaping up to be even longer. But you know…maybe we'll see each other again. Soon, too."

"Yeah, I hope so."

"It was great meeting you, Frank," Roosevelt said. Smiling, he said, "I think maybe we'll see you again sooner rather than later."

Ava cringed, but if that was the most embarrassing comment her father had let loose on them tonight, she considered herself lucky. She opened the door and followed Frank outside into the hall. They walked a few steps down the hallway so any prying ears wouldn't hear their conversation.

"So, that was fun," Frank said. "And dinner was delicious."

"Good, I was afraid this quickly thrown-together dinner was going to be almost laughable."

"Not at all." He stepped closer to her and held her gaze. "I did feel like this might have been a test—a way for you to test the waters to see if they were ready for you to move on."

"In all fairness, I think it was."

He nodded and said, "Well, if I may be so blunt, I believe I passed. But that leaves one remaining question: are *you* ready to move on?"

"I want to be. But I feel like I'm betraying him. I feel like…shit, I don't know."

"I won't rush you, Ava. I'm falling for you. There's no sense in me pretending otherwise. So just take whatever time you need and let me know when…or *if* you're ever ready."

Their eyes were still locked, and she could feel everything in her body being pulled towards him. She forced herself to look away, staring down at the floor.

"What is it?" he asked. "Did I say something wrong?"

"No. It's just that I'm finding it very hard not to kiss you right now."

Frank chuckled nervously. "Then kiss me."

She looked back up to him, her eyes brimming with tears. "I can't. Not yet."

He reached out and took her hand. "It's okay." He then pulled her close and placed a soft kiss on her forehead. Then, with a smile, he said, "Goodnight, Ava."

He turned away, the smile still on his face, and she watched him go. It was an odd feeling because the knowledge that she'd see him again tomorrow made her anxious for the next day. And when she finally walked back into her apartment, she realized that her heart felt as if it were overflowing. Everything was going to be okay. So long as she took her time and didn't rush into things, the world was filled with possibilities—in work, in family, and in love.

It was almost enough to make her think that a full of acceptance of her place within police department might be around the corner. Of course, things with the department were never easy to predict, and that was something she knew she had to keep in mind before she allowed herself to feel too confident in the course her life was going.

CHAPTER FOUR

The positive feelings carried over to the following morning but quickly started to dissipate as she walked into the precinct. Ever since she'd shed light on dirty cops during her last case, there had been a palpable tension in the air every time she walked through or around the bullpen at work. Faces that were once supportive or at least indifferent to her now seemed hostile. As she made her way through the building, she glanced quickly over to Frank's desk and saw it empty. The coffee cup, still steaming, told her that he was in, just somewhere else—likely speaking with Minard or in Records. Without that bit of familiarity and shelter available to her, she hurried to the stairs.

Even simply walking to the Women's Bureau offices downstairs made her feel shielded from the animosity upstairs. There were four women in the room, two of whom Ava had still not gotten to know. The other two, though, had become fast friends and Ava often found herself wishing that they would be given the same chances she'd been offered.

Frances, the head of the Women's Division, was currently clacking away at her beast of a typewriter. The hammering of the keys sounded like gunfire. A few paces away from Frances, Lottie was pushing her chair behind her desk. She had on a light coat and a hat, a telltale sign that she was heading out on a case—a rarity for Lottie.

"Good morning, ladies," Ava said.

"Ladies?" Lottie said with a smile. She had a radiant glow to her when she smiled, and Ava often wondered if Lottie might be a little too pretty to be a policewoman. She could only imagine the sort of catcalls and whistles Lottie got while out on the beat. "There are no ladies here!"

"No?" Ava asked, going along with the joke.

"Nope. Why, just this morning, I was called *sweet thing* and a *harlot*. All within the span of five minutes, mind you. The men in this city…I tell you. They could learn some manners."

"Are you off to teach them some?"

"Of course not. Apparently, the only thing us gals are capable of is following up on run-away orphans. We got a report about a murdered female immigrant come across this morning but apparently that's too high-profile for us." Lottie shrugged as she made her way to the exit. "Run-away orphans sure as hell beat wasting away in this office, though."

Lottie gave a little wave as she left. Ava walked over to where Frances was slipping a sheet of paper off the roller of the typewriter. She was filling out arrest reports from male officers that had made arrests the night before and had since knocked off from their shift. Ava thought she'd find such work almost demeaning, but Frances had always seemed to take such things in stride. It was likely why she was in charge of the WB.

"A murdered immigrant?" Ava asked. "Who's running with that?"

Frances gave a tired little laugh and shook her head. "No one. A broke immigrant woman on the shit-side of town. No one is taking it."

"So we're just going to let it go?"

"Yeah. It happens more than you might think. As more and more immigrants start coming in, the police tend to pay less and less attention to violent crimes against them. Now if those crimes affect people a little closer to home, that's a different story."

"Well, that's disheartening."

"It is." Frances gave a small shrug, as if to say: *What are you gonna do?*

It was enough to dampen the overall sense of security she often felt in the WB offices, so she gave Frances a quick goodbye and then headed back upstairs. She figured if Frank wasn't back at his desk yet, she's talk to Minard and see if there was anything she could do to help find the immigrant woman's killer.

When she came to the top of the stairs, she saw that Frank's desk *was* still empty. She knew it was a little self-obsessed, but there was a small part of her that couldn't help but wonder any time Frank was away if he was being lectured by Minard about her performance. She hated to feel like every single thing was about her, but because her career started the way it had, it was very easy to get hung up in such thoughts.

Apparently, the morning's staring-session had come to an end— either that or no one had seen her come back up the stairs. Ava was able to make it over to Captain Minard's office without anyone staring daggers at her. And when she knocked on the door, she was pleased to hear that Minard sounded as if his morning had gone well. She knew his voice through the door well enough now to be able to read his mood based on its tone.

"Come on in!"

When she opened the door, she wasn't really all that surprised to see Frank in the office. He sat in one of the two chairs in front of Minard's desk. The other was occupied by an officer by the name of Simmons. When he saw Ava come in, he looked away quickly. He got to his feet and nodded to Minard.

"Thanks for hearing me out, Captain," Simmons said. When he headed for the door, he sidestepped Ava without so much as acknowledging her presence.

"By the way, sir," Frank said. "That's exactly what I'm talking about."

"What?" Ava asked. "What have you been talking about?"

"Detective Wimbly has been telling me just how rude most of the force has been to you over the past few days."

"It's nothing, really."

"No, it is," Frank said. "In the past few weeks, you've done a significant amount more than any man out there. And yet you're still seen as this…this…*pariah!* If it's an issue with you being a woman, they need to get over it. And if it's something else—"

"Hold your tone," Minard told Frank. "I've taken note of your complaints and will look into it."

"And what did Simmons want?" Ava asked.

"Something unrelated," Minard said. He looked to both of them and then opened his empty hands to them. "I've got nothing for you today. Not yet, anyway. It's been rather slow. I can send you on patrols, maybe have you run by a few banks to check on security. With the news about the financial sector not looking so good, I imagine moods and tempers have got to be steaming in some of the banks."

"If you don't mind me saying so," Ava said, "there's something else I'd like to look into."

"What's that?"

"Frances and Lottie were telling me about the murder of an immigrant somewhere on the Lower East Side. Apparently, no one thought it was important enough to look into."

"Most don't," he said. "And not just out of the precinct."

"Well, you said yourself there's nothing else going on right now."

"Gold, you've done well—better than anyone expected, if we're honest. But you still need to know your place. You can't request certain cases you want to take on."

"This isn't even a case if no one has looked into it. Sir, it's not fair. My grandmother was an immigrant from Ireland. I know the hard times she had. My mother, too. We all came from somewhere else, sir. I don't understand why it's all of a sudden a negative thing. All I ask is for the chance to look into it. If something more pressing comes along, I'll back off."

Minard sighed and looked at Frank. "Thoughts?"

"I think a woman has been killed and we don't know who did it. As detectives, that's pretty much our job, sir."

"Fine," Minard said without much thought or hesitation. "Look into it. But as soon as you even get the scent that it's nothing more than a hate crime against a potentially illegal immigrant, I want your backsides back in this precinct."

"Is there any paperwork at all, sir?" Ava asked.

"Just the report that was sent down to Frances. And it equates to nothing more than 'female immigrant found dead in alley.' Check with her. She can at least give you the location."

Another thing Ava had learned about Captain Minard was to know when to take your leave. She did so then, not wanting to give him another second to rethink his answer. She left the office with Frank hurrying out behind her, assigned to a case that no one else found interesting enough to pursue.

CHAPTER FIVE

"I didn't know that about your family," Frank said. "That your grandmother was an immigrant from Ireland."

"Yeah. My family has always done okay, I suppose. My grandmother came over here rather wealthy. But a lot of the money was squandered, I think. My family wasn't the sort to talk about a lot of their history. My father sort of avoids it at all costs."

"Did you ever know your grandmother?"

"Barely. She died when I was young. I have a few memories, though."

"And what about your mother? Somehow, we've never—"

"Not while we're working," she said with a smile, interrupting him. "Save that talk for the next dinner."

"And when might that be?"

She didn't answer as they walked into the back lot. Frank walked to the patrol car he'd been favoring as of late, slipping in behind the wheel. When he started the car and pulled out into morning traffic, Ava found herself settling into an odd sort of comfort. She and Frank had been partners long enough for her to feel comfortable with him, but there was also the blossoming romantic angle to their relationship, too. It was one of the areas where those different aspects of her life merged, giving her hope that at some point in the future, they could all coexist.

"This immigrant problem,' Frank said as he drove, "shouldn't really even be a problem. It's the prejudice of the people that live around here that is the problem. I don't see how this city—hell, this *country*—is supposed to be such a beacon of hope when it treats newcomers from different backgrounds like dirt." He looked to her a bit guilty and added: "Not that you asked for my opinion on the matter."

"When did it originally become such a problem?"

"Depends on who you ask. But we started getting reports of murders and abuse at a pretty steady rate about two years ago. If you want another free opinion, I think it's mainly because people are really worried about this looming financial disaster. People are so worried someone else might make a dime that they could be making."

Ava said nothing about it; it seemed beyond selfish to her but at some core level, she thought she understood it. As they finished up the drive to the crime scene, she thought about what it must be like for immigrants, coming to a new place off of a boat shared with others that had the same dreams and aspirations. There was a vulnerability to it that she was quite sure she could never reach, a sense of throwing caution and life to the wind and praying that you ended up in a stable and safe place. It made her even more sympathetic to immigrants which probably wasn't the best thing, considering where they were currently headed and the case they were currently on.

When Frank parked in front of the tenement listed on the brief crime report, Ava realized that it truly did seem like a different world on this side of the city. The apartment buildings looked poorly maintained even from the outside, and there was trash and other street debris cluttering the sidewalks. When they stepped out, she also noticed a stench in the air, tinged with what she was pretty sure was human excrement.

"These buildings don't have indoor plumbing, do they?"

"No. Some of them don't even have running water from what I understand."

It made Ava feel a bit spoiled as they skipped the tenement altogether and walked to the alley where the woman—listed as Eve Buzek—had been murdered. It was nothing more than a thin walkway between two tenement buildings. She guessed it to be about five feet wide, and that five feet of space was filled with crisscrossing clotheslines. There seemed to be no real order to the lines, most of which were heavy with drying clothes and sheets.

"Well, one thing is for sure," Ava said, peering into the alleyway. "With this maze of clotheslines, there's no way she would have been seen from the street. Not unless every single one of these clotheslines was empty at the time."

She found the mere idea of all the lines being empty slightly ridiculous. It was almost dizzying to look as far back as she could. She could see the end of the alleyway much further back, but even back there it consisted of more lines and hanging clothes.

"That means the killer would have had ample opportunity to hide," Frank pointed out.

As they walked slowly into the alleyway, Ava heard footsteps further ahead. Dodging several articles of torn clothing and stained, threadbare sheets, they went deeper into the alley. A little less than halfway down, they saw a girl of about thirteen hanging clothes from one of the lines. The faint smell of soap was barely strong enough to break through the still-lingering smell of human waste.

The girl saw the two detectives and stopped moving, her hands reaching into a dented bucket of freshly washed clothes. She froze for a moment and, to Ava, looked like a frightened animal in the wild that was spooked by a sudden appearance in its habitat.

"It's okay," Ava said, keeping her voice soft and moderately cheerful. "We're only here because we're hoping to solve a crime that was committed here."

The girl barely nodded, her hands still unmoving in the bucket of clothes. She slowly turned her head, as if looking for an adult presence to step into what was clearly a stressful situation for her.

"It really is okay," Ava said. "We're not here for trouble. We're detectives—policemen."

The little girl squinted her eyes and tilted her head. "But you're a woman."

Even to poor immigrants the idea of a notable female detective seems strange, Ava thought. It was pretty disheartening.

"I am," Ava said. "My name is Ava, and the man right here with me is Frank. We're here to see if we can find out who killed the woman that lived here just yesterday."

The girl finally took her hands out of the bucket, bringing with them a pair of tattered pants. "Do you mean Eve?"

"Yes, that's right," Ava said. "Eve Buzek. Did you know her?"

"Yes. She was very nice. She always made me laugh."

Frank stepped forward and when he spoke, he also kept his voice as cheerful as he could. It didn't quite fit him, but the girl didn't seem to notice. "Did you live with Eve?" Frank asked.

"No, sir. I live here, in this building." She nodded to the building to her right as she hung up the pants. "Eve lived in this one," she added, now nodding to the building on her left.

"I don't suppose you know what happened to her, do you?" Ava asked.

"No. I didn't even know she'd been killed until last night. My Momma told me Eve had been killed and that I needed to be very careful whenever I stepped out of the building."

Ava turned to look at the building Eve had called home and noticed a small wooden door on the side slowly opening. It opened just a crack, and she caught sight of two children peering out. One of them, a young girl of about four or five, smiled at her and then dashed away. The second, a boy that appeared to be around ten years of age, looked out with wide eyes.

"Hello there," Ava said to the boy. "Do you live here?"

The boy nodded. He opened the door a bit wider, revealing more of his face. There were nicks and scratches on his cheeks, and dirt patches all around, mostly on his forehead. His dark hair was greasy and matted.

"Are your parents home?"

"Yes…my father."

"We'd like to speak with him," Frank said. He stepped forward and showed the kid his badge as if he were pulling off a magic trick.

The boy's eyes grew wider as he opened the door. Frank took the lead; Ava had been the clear choice to speak with the spooked girl but Frank was the go-to for men that were most likely not going to respect her position of authority. Also, the inside of the apartment building was filled with shadows and looked like an invitation to some kind of disaster. While Frank was fully aware of Ava's tenacity and capability to take care of herself, he still stepped in as the role of protector most of the time. Ava did not feel that it was necessary, but she did appreciate it.

The interior of the apartment was worse than Ava had imagined. First of all, it was a stretch to call it an apartment. The room they walked into was one large open space, with just a single room partitioned off in the back. That room, she barely saw, gave way to a lot of small cubby-like areas that she assumed served as rooms. On the other side, there was a rickety wooden staircase that led upstairs, the landing of which was visible by what looked like nothing more than a torn area in the ceiling.

But it was the central area that kept her attention—not only because it was so disgusting, but because there were five people cluttered around it. Two were sitting on overturned buckets, in the middle of a card game. The young girl that had been peeking out into the alley was sitting on the bare wooden floor, looking at a yellowed and well-worn picture book. Two other children in the pre-teen age range were huddled on filthy blankets that had been spread out on the floor. And all around it, the smell of sweat, piss, and God only knew what else, was thick and pungent.

The wide-eyed boy dashed over to one of the card players. "Daddy! This man is a cop!"

Both card players eyed Frank suspiciously. One of them, the boy's father, then stared at Ava as if he were trying to devour her with his eyes. He was wearing a stained white shirt and pants that looked as if they may rot away after another few washes. The man's face was just as filthy as his son's and he was rail thin. He said nothing at first, his eyes still locked on Ava.

Noticing this, Frank stepped in front of him. "That's enough of that, sir."

"What the bloody hell are cops doing here?" the father asked.

"We're trying to find out who killed Eve Buzek."

"Is that so? Are the police finally starting to give a damn about what happens in this neck of the woods?"

"Did you know Eve?" Frank asked, ignoring the man's jab.

"I did. She lived here, back there," he pointed to the room that led to the small, divided spaces in the back.

"How long did you know her?" Ava asked. "Were you related?"

"No. As far as I know, she didn't have no family other than her father. They moved in here just a few days after me and my family did."

"And what about her father?"

"No clue. I haven't seen him in a few days. He and Eve were close, though. I can't even imagine what he must be going through."

Ava thought back to the flimsy report and could not recall seeing anything about Eve's father. She doubted the police that came to the scene initially even bothered looking for family or next of kin. Eve was just an immigrant; what was the point?

"And how long was she here, sharing this space with you?" Frank asked.

The man shrugged. He was so skinny and malnourished that Ava could see his collarbones rise and fall as he did so. "A few months. Maybe three? I'm not sure. All the days sort of run together out here, you know?"

"Do you know if Eve had any enemies? People that hated her or had something against her?"

"No. Everyone seemed to like her. But if you don't mind my saying, I don't know if you need to be looking for someone that didn't like her. I think you might want to be looking for someone that liked her a little too much. Eve was very pretty and very friendly. I'd seen and heard more than a few men proposition her, offering her money for…well, for certain things."

"Did she ever accept those offers?" Ava asked.

"Not as far as I know. But that don't mean nothing. The things that go on out on those alleys…it would keep your police force busy forever. Just because she turned those men down don't mean they took 'no' for an answer."

This disgusted Ava and again made her feel incredibly privileged. She was far from living in the lap of luxury in the apartment she and Clarence had barely been able to afford, but as she heard these stories while standing in this filthy room, she almost felt like a queen.

"Sir, do you know who found Eve's body?"

"Nope."

"Were there any witnesses?" Frank asked. "Did anyone hear her scream or cry out for help?"

The father looked to them with a new sort of skepticism. Ava knew even before things went any farther that this man was done talking to them and she suspected she knew why. They were pressing hard about the death of an innocent woman—a woman this man claimed had been quite pretty. Perhaps he felt that their being here was because an attractive woman had died. But where had the police been when immigrants of all ages, appearances, and backgrounds had been suffering? That, in tandem with the barrage of questions they were throwing at him, might have him feeling nervous. And based on the way the police had treated these people in the past, she didn't really blame him.

"Are you going to answer the question?" Frank asked.

"Sorry. I don't understand you. I don't speak English so well." His tone was rough, but there was a soft sort of resignation on his face. Ava thought he *wanted* to help them as much as he could but was starting to worry about why they might really be there and how it could affect the lives of other immigrants. She wanted to plead with him that they were genuinely there to help but knew it would do no good. The man's mind had already been made up.

"What?" Frank asked. "You were just speaking to me!"

The father shrugged. Frank started forward, but Ava reached out and took his arm. She shook her head and led him slowly back to the door. Every set of eyes in the room watched them make their exit as they stepped back out into the alley.

"What do you think that guy was playing at?" Frank asked.

"I think he's under the impression that we're only here because a pretty woman was murdered. And I don't think they have a very high opinion of cops…or anyone in any position of power actually. And can you blame them? They're getting the short end of the stick out here."

Frank sighed and looked down the alleyway. The young girl that had been hanging laundry was gone, her load of clothes dripping onto the pavement.

"Well, you wanted the case," Frank said. "If we're going to allow these people to pretend that they know nothing, where do we go from here?"

"Let's see if Eve has anything to tell us," she said, walking back to the car. "I think we should take a trip to the coroner."

CHAPTER SIX

The stubborn father back at the tenement building had been right; Eve Buzek had been very pretty indeed. It was a fact that was plain to see, but it did bother Ava that she was not as bothered by the sight of the woman's corpse as she thought she should be. There were no clear signs of death or abuse at first. As she and Frank looked at the body on the coroner's slab, Ava felt as if they were simply looking at a perfect specimen of the female body. If not for the bruises along her neck, Ava would have been puzzled as to the cause of death.

"So what is it you're looking for, exactly?" the coroner asked. He was a chubby man with a well-polished moustache and a pair of half-moon glasses perched in front of his eyes.

"Anything we can get," Ava said. "Cause of death, any clues the killer might have left behind, any signs as to what sort of life she might have been leading."

"Well, the cause of death was most definitely strangulation. But if you take a look at her neck right there, you can see that the bruising doesn't line up with any typical signs of being strangled."

Ava was, quite honestly, not certain what the typical signs of strangulation looked like outside of harsh bruising. But she noted Frank nodding, stepping closer and leaning in a bit to get a closer look. "Yeah, what is that? There's something there…circular almost. A noose, maybe?"

"Doubtful," the coroner said. "There are no rope fibers, and almost every single time I've ever seen evidence of a hanging—which has been far too often—there are places along the flesh that have been rubbed raw from the rope. No, this strangling was done with something soft. Maybe a scarf or a sheet."

"Makes sense," Ava said. "If the killer attacked in the alley, perhaps she was also doing laundry. That sorry excuse for a report never mentioned it, right?"

"Yeah," Frank said. He nodded to the front of the Eve's neck. "There's definitely more pressure applied here at the front. He likely pulled from behind, right?"

"Yes, that's my theory," the coroner said. "And if it's a correct theory, whoever was behind her was quite strong. You can tell by the way the bruising gets darker right along the curvature of the neck on the sides."

"We're having trouble trying to figure out anything about her," Ava said. "During your examination, did you find any clues that might tell us *anything* about her?"

"Not much, really. Because strangulation is clearly the cause of death, there's been no autopsy, of course. I did, however, find a rather interesting substance in her hair. It was a powder that I could not quite identify at first; it was so fine, I thought maybe it was just dandruff. But it had a very pleasant smell to it. It took me a while to realize that it was powdered detergent."

"You mean like soap?" Frank asked.

"I thought so at first, but it was quite grainy. I thought it might mean she did an excessive amount of laundry."

This struck Ava as odd. Sure, all they knew of Eve was that she had died in the alley where there were a lot of clothes being hung to dry. But an immigrant with no money wasn't going to be able to afford such a detergent. Curious, she looked to Eve's hands—her fingers in particular. They looked rather red, the skin almost chapped. Feeling very strange doing so, she leaned closer and smelled them.

"I think she was working with laundry," Ava said. "And not just her own. I think she was doing it as a job. Her fingers look like they're shriveled and red—pretty common for washing clothes over and over again. And the detergent…there's no way she would be able to afford that. From what I understand, most immigrants use the same soap to wash their bodies and their clothes—if anything at all. An industrial detergent like this likely wasn't used for personal use."

"So I guess we'll look at local industrial laundry services," Frank said.

"There aren't many of those that I know of. We'd need to run a search for ones that might be willing to hire immigrants."

Frank thought about it for a moment and eventually shrugged. "I don't know that anyone would admit to that."

They both looked to the dead woman one more time before giving their thanks to the coroner. On the way out, Ava again found herself wondering if there might be some other reason an immigrant woman would have been so close to cleaning products and washing so much that it had visibly affected her hands. She agreed with Frank that no one would likely admit to hiring an immigrant but on the other hand, it might be a smart move by a business. They could pay immigrants next to nothing and probably do it all under the table.

"I guess we just start looking for industrial cleaners from this point, right?" Frank asked. They were leaving the coroner's office, Frank holding the door open for her.

"Yeah, I think so. There can't be that many, right?"

"I don't know. I know there are a few that work only with hotels—doing their sheets and all. But other than that, I don't know if—"

"Excuse me," a woman said from behind them. "Detectives?"

They both turned around and saw an old woman. She was very short in stature and the clothes she was wearing looked like nothing more than rags. At first, Ava thought she might be as old as ninety, but a closer look revealed that the grime and slightly discolored skin on her face had given that impression. Underneath it all, she was probably closer to sixty.

"What is it, ma'am?" Frank asked, clearly trying to make it appear as if they were in a hurry.

"You were back at the tenements earlier, yes? Looking into Eve's death?"

"Yes," Ava said. "How did you know that?"

"I live in the neighboring building—the one across from where Eve lived. You spoke to my granddaughter for a bit."

"The girl that was hanging clothes?"

"Yes. I could not speak to you there because many of the people that live in those buildings don't trust the police. If I was seen talking to you, they'd turn their backs on me. And as you can imagine, we have to work to support one another in order to get by."

"I understand," Ava said. "Did you know Eve?"

"I did. Very much. She was a very sweet girl."

"Ma'am, we don't really have much information on her. Is there anything at all that you can tell us about her? Was she, by any chance, working with someone that gave her a job doing laundry?"

"Recently, yes. But before that she did anything she could manage. She was a textile worker for a while, and then a ship-scrubber down at the docks but I believe she quit that after so many men continued to be inappropriate with her."

"Was she working with this laundry company when she died?" Frank asked.

"Yes. She seemed to enjoy it, even though she knew she was being paid substantially less than most of the other women there."

"Would you happen to know where this place is located?" Ava asked.

"I don't have a name or anything, but I know it was down on Hester Street. She told me one day when she tried to convince me to get a job there."

Ava neatly tucked that bit of useful information away and wanted to hurry off to find the laundry outfit in question. After all, Hester Street wasn't too far away. But she also knew a resource like this old lady wasn't likely to come along again anytime soon. Frank also knew these things, and they usually came to him a bit faster than they came to Ava. She supposed it came down to experience.

"Ma'am," Frank said, "Do you know any of the people she lives with?"

"Not well. The kids living in her building will often come to our building, and the other way around, to play. I've seen some of the other family members in passing, but we do not know one another well."

"Do you think it might be possible that someone Eve lived with may have killed her?"

"I wondered that myself, but I don't think so. As I said…we may not be the most well-knit community, but we rely on each other. There is no real help to be had for us anywhere else." She looked away quickly, as if she thought she may have accidentally insulted them. "In other words, I do not think it would be practical for one of our own to kill another. Especially not one that is so good at playing with and speaking to the children."

"You followed us here to speak with us," Ava said. "Right? Do you know something that might help us?"

"Well, that's just it. I know nothing. But I'm damned tired of immigrants dying and no one caring. Some starve, others get sick and can't afford medicine. Some get beat or killed by drunks and nothing is being done about it. So I wanted to help, hoping the little bit I do know about Eve might be useful."

"Well, it certainly has," Frank said. "We left the coroner with no clear direction and you've given us a street to start from. You may have saved us about half a day of useless searching. So thank you for that." He then looked around quickly, as if he were about to tell a secret and wanted no one to see him doing it; he reached into his pocket. He pulled out a single dollar bill and handed it to the woman. "Get yourself something to eat. And thank you for your help."

The woman did not take the money right away. She looked at it skeptically and Ava was pretty certain that woman thought Frank might be playing a trick on her. But he thrust it closer to her and she finally took it. She nodded and stuffed it into what served as a pocket on the ratty old pants she was wearing.

"Thank you," she said, still seeming uncertain about the gift. She then shuffled off quickly, maybe afraid the kind detective would change his mind.

"That was very kind of you," Ava said. "But isn't it a rule that we aren't supposed to give people money or handouts?"

"It's a loose rule for sure. But if others can get away with using money to bribe the mob for information, I think it's okay to use a single dollar to help an old, needy woman to eat. Still…maybe don't tell anyone else."

"That you're kind or that you gave her the money?"

Frank smirked at her as they got back into the patrol car. "Both."

Frank got behind the wheel as Ava slid into the passenger seat. With nothing more than a potential work location for an employer that may not even admit Eve had worked there, they continued on with a case no one seemed to have wanted in the first place—a case Ava couldn't help but feel had a simple answer hiding somewhere in these neglected, dirty streets. And now, thanks to an immigrant, they had a lead to work with.

CHAPTER SEVEN

As far as they could tell, there was only one laundry business on Hester Street. It was located at the very end of a block that consisted of small businesses that all seemed to be new and barely hanging on. Ava couldn't help but wonder what the looming financial situation might do to those businesses, and it made the already gray and forlorn street seem even more hopeless.

When they stepped in through the front door, the heat and strong smell of detergent and soap was nearly overwhelming. The building was really not much more than a large, open room. The only two things that broke up the open space were wooden columns that helped hold up the ceiling, a thin and ill-constructed temporary wall that hid away most of the laundry area from the front of the building, and a single desk sitting up front.

The desk was empty when Ava and Frank approached it. A bell sat on the desk, along with a ledger and nothing else. Assuming the bell was there for a reason, Ava reached out and dinged it. It was a loud, thin noise that seemed to rocket through the building. A response came right away in a high, shrill, and slightly irritated voice from behind the wall.

"One moment, please!"

"At least we'll leave here smelling good," Frank joked.

Ava wasn't so sure about that. The smell of so much potent detergent was getting to her, stinging her eyes and nostrils. As she started to get used to it, she realized that it was an intensified version of what she'd smelled on Eve Buzek's fingers. As she mulled this over and waited for the woman behind the wall to show up, she and Frank stood among the scents and sounds of water sloshing about and fabric being cleaned. It was an oddly satisfying sound and if not for the strong smell filling the place, she may have found it peaceful.

Finally, a woman came around the wall and hurried over to the desk. Her blonde hair was up, but many wet tendrils had spilled down. She was sweating, giving her an almost angelic glow and when she smiled, it was clear it was one of necessity, not cheer.

"What can I do for you fine folks today?" the woman asked.

Ava could tell that Frank was waiting for her to show her badge first. They'd both come to understand over the course of their brief partnership that women were impressed by a woman with a badge. Most of the time, it seemed to also steer the women toward being agreeable and as helpful as possible.

Ava showed her badge and, putting on the same sort of rehearsed sneer as the laundress had moments ago, she said: "I'm Detective Gold and this is my partner, Frank Wimbly. We're here to ask about a woman we believe works here. Or, rather, *worked* here."

"And who might that be?" the sweating woman asked.

In asking this question, Ava thought she detected an accent of some kind. Irish, maybe? She couldn't be sure. It made her wonder if this woman might also be an immigrant.

"Eve Buzek."

"Yeah? What about her?"

"Well, I don't know if you've been informed yet or not, but she was found dead just outside of her home. It appears she was murdered."

"Eve? Dead?" The woman looked both puzzled and shocked. She looked sad, too, but not near tears.

"Yes. I'm sorry to be the one to tell you. But all we were able to really learn about her is that she worked here. I assume that's correct?"

"Yes. She worked here—with me a lot of the time." She spoke slowly, still processing the news.

"Was she well liked?"

"Yes, by everyone." She looked behind her, making sure no one was listening in, and leaned a bit closer to the detectives. "Our boss was a little hard on her sometimes, but she's hard on everyone."

"What's your name?" Ava asked.

"Marie."

"How long have you worked here, Marie?"

Marie thought about it for a moment and shrugged. "Maybe two months."

"And how long have you been in the country?"

"Less than five months. I came over from Ireland with my sister and my mother."

Ava nodded, looking back over at the wall that hid away most of the workers. She could see a few women sitting on wooden stools and hunched over wash bins and basins. "How many immigrants are working here?"

Marie let out a little nervous laugh. "Most of us are. We can—"

Behind Ava and Frank, the door they had entered through opened up. A woman, very prim and proper, eyed the situation furtively. She was tall and quite pretty, maybe middle-aged. She wore a dress that probably cost more than any woman behind the wall made in the course of an entire month.

"What's this?" the woman said. "What's going on here? Marie…get back to work!"

"These detectives rang the bell and I—"

"Back to work, I said!" She did not really even raise her voice, but it *seemed* like she did. She just had that sort of voice.

Marie did as she was asked, giving Ava and Frank one last glance before she hurried back behind the wall to take up her station. Meanwhile, the tall woman—presumably the manager or owner—made her way around the desk and stared the detectives down. "So. You're detectives?" She looked at Ava as she said this, clearly finding it hard to believe.

"Yes," Ava said, again showing her badge. She felt an overwhelming urge to pelt the woman with it, but restrained herself.

"Yes," Frank echoed. "Yes, we are. And we're here to ask about a woman that works here. A woman that was killed yesterday."

"Killed? Who was it?"

"Eve Buzek. She was killed in an alley beside her home."

"If she was killed at her home, why are you here? I don't need the police snooping around my place! It's bad for business."

"We just want to ask you a few questions about Eve," Ava said.

"I knew nothing about her. I hire these women to work, not to make friends. Now, please…I need you to leave before someone sees you here."

Ava noted that the woman looked upset but couldn't peg why. "But you do know who she was?"

"Of course I do. She was…well, she was kind. Always making others laugh. But that's all I know."

"You seem to want us out of here quickly," Frank said. "Would that happen to be because you have a large group of immigrants behind that wall, some of whom may not be here legally?"

"No! I would never!"

The reaction was so dramatic that Ava was certain she was lying. "Well then, how about this?" she said. "You be honest and tell us what you know about Eve without trying to rush us out and we won't go back there asking questions. Does that work?"

The woman looked relieved but also aggravated. She'd been bested with a simple request and had no way of responding without either cooperating or getting herself into trouble. She sighed and asked: "What do you want to know?"

"Anything you can tell us. We know nothing about her, we only figured out she worked here because of traces of detergent in her hair at the coroner's office."

"Like I said…she was always good for a laugh. It was almost sad in a way because you could tell she wasn't truly happy. But she made the most out of every day. She made a lot of friends back there with the other women. I…well, I came to like her quite a bit."

"Friends," Ava said, "So she had people to talk to?"

"Yes. She was so happy to find work here…not to make too much of myself. She had previously worked at a textile mill, and they were paying her terribly. No breaks, twelve hour shifts six days a week. So, when she got here and saw people that actually cared about her and keeping a somewhat upbeat workplace, you could tell she appreciated it."

"Can you think of any reason someone might want her dead?" Frank asked.

"I really can't. Not at all. She was a pleasant young woman that, given time, could have really made something of herself if she really stuck to her guns."

"Did you ever talk to her outside of work?"

The woman nodded slowly, and Ava could see that she was legitimately troubled by the news of Eve's death. "Yes. There are a few women that live in questionable parts of the city. If you've seen where Eve lived, you know what I'm talking about. Sometimes, I walk home with the girls and then take a cab home. I walked with Eve a few times. Three times…maybe four. I can't quite recall. She had a particularly nasty walk home. There were these men, this riled-up group of men that were self-proclaimed anti-immigrant soldiers. They really gave her a hard time."

This didn't seem to make sense at first. After all, Ava had just seen the way she spoke with Marie. She wondered if it was some sort of an act—either pretending to be a bad-ass broad to certain women in the back or wanting the general public to think she was coming down hard on her workers at all times. She also wondered if it was just a defense mechanism she used because she was a female business-owner in a city ruled by men.

"Did you encounter these men on any of your walks with her?" Frank asked.

"Yes. Just once, though. They were just sitting on a porch stoop, like they were waiting for her—her or any other immigrant. It was mostly harmless insults, but there were a few very vulgar comments, too. Things I'd really rather not repeat if it's all the same to you."

"Do you think they would go through with any of their comments, or was it just talk?" Frank asked.

"I truly don't know," the woman said. "I think about that very thing sometimes. I like to think no one could be so cruel, but there was just so much hatred in the way they acted. I…I really don't know."

"Do you remember where this stoop was where they were hanging out?" Frank asked.

"I do," she said. "Regrettably, there are many more little groups like that in the city, though." She eyed them with sadness in her eyes. "I pay them fairly," she said. "I won't lie; I don't pay them as well as I'd pay a local. Not at first, anyway. But I have women back there that were able to get out of squalor with the money they made here. I'm not running an illegal shop, but…"

She shrugged here, and Ava gathered what she meant. *She* wasn't running things illegally, but there might be a few girls working in the back that weren't legally in the city. And as far as Ava was concerned, that was very minor in the grand scheme of things.

"Can we get that address?" Ava asked quickly, just in case Frank decided to ask her what she meant, exactly.

"It was less than fifteen minutes from where she lived, down on Donner Street. There's a small string of apartment buildings across the street from a grocer's shop. That's where they were."

"Thank you," Ava said. She felt she should say something else, perhaps how she didn't have to put on a hard façade when there were strangers around. If she was legitimately being kind to these immigrant women, that was something to be applauded, not scoffed at.

It was also a sign that not everyone in this city hated immigrants. And though it seemed small in the moment, Ava wondered if there were any other kind souls out there that may be able to help provide them with some answers.

CHAPTER EIGHT

Frank was driving back in the direction of the immigrant side of the Lower East Side. He really seemed to be much more comfortable behind the wheel of an auto now; Ava found herself letting out little yelps and bracing her feet against the floorboard much less these days.

"I'm going to go ahead and say this," Frank said. "It may seem crude but you're going to need to get used to these sorts of theories and approaches on cases like these."

"You're wondering that if Eve was attacked by someone that hated immigrants that much, why wasn't she raped. Right?"

"Yeah. And it sounded a lot less rude coming out of your mouth for some reason."

"I was thinking about it, too. If Eve *was* attacked by a member of an anti-immigrant group that was shouting vulgar things at her, I think there would at least be a good possibility that he'd also sexually abuse her."

"All men don't resort to that, though," Frank argued. "I know it makes little sense but somr men will draw the line at beating the hell out of a woman. By some skewed religious viewpoint, beating and abusing a woman is almost accepted. But rape…that's a whole different thing. I'm not saying I agree with that line of thought, but it's more common than you think."

"So in other words, you think the absence of sexual abuse doesn't mean that we can automatically let even a small part of our guard up when it comes to this group."

"That's right." He let out a deep breath and looked over to her. "If you and I are going to explore anything between us, I guess I need to be honest with you. This whole surplus of immigrants thing…it does bug me. I do think there are far too many people flooding into the city from across the sea. But I'm not one of these men that are thinking it's some huge injustice to the locals. And sadly, there aren't many others like that on the force right now."

She nodded as she looked through the windshield, watching the city roll by. "Well, thanks for that honesty. The immigrant issue doesn't really bother me. I think it says a lot about New York and maybe even the entire country, that so many want to come here. It may seem selfish, but it makes me feel secure in a weird way."

That vulnerable exchange hung between them as they neared Donner Street. Unable to take the silence and the weight of the moment, Ava asked a question that had been nagging at her ever since they'd seen the alley where Eve had been killed.

"She was strangled with a sheet or some sort of cloth. Maybe even a piece of her own. Does that make you think it was premeditated or just an act of hatred or passion that the murderer just couldn't pass up?"

"It's hard to say. But I lean towards premeditation. It's pretty rare that a murder committed out of the rage or passion of a moment is done with something to aid the killer—a gun, a knife, or a noose, for example. Those are usually murders that involve lots of violence, and blood. Being strangled from behind—with or without the assistance of a sheet or some other cloth—seems to speak of premeditation as far as I'm concerned."

"And premeditation likely lends itself to coming from a group that is fueled by a shared hatred, wouldn't you say?"

Frank grinned and nodded. "That sounds pretty deep. But yes, that's my own personal opinion."

They came upon Donner Street a bit faster than Ava had expected. She scanned the street as Frank found the grocer's shop the woman back at the laundry had mentioned. When he parked along the curb, Ava could see the odd transition of appearances in the neighborhood. It was a huge step up from the squalor of the tenements they'd visited earlier in the day but would still be considered the ghetto or the slums by most of the officers back at the precinct. As she took it all in, she saw something a block over on the other side of the street that seemed to almost invite them.

"Look at that, would you?" she said, finding their luck a little hard to believe.

Roughly a dozen people were gathered on the street, forming two lines. Almost all of them had signs made of wood or butcher's paper. Ava could see two of them clearly from where she stood as she got out of the car. One read: **NY is NOT a home for all!** The second one read: **Save jobs for locals!!!**

They'd arrived just in time to watch an anti-immigrant protest get started. Because Ava had considered her own heritage recently when asked about it, she found the very idea of this protest ill-informed and somewhat ignorant. Did these protesters not understand that every single one of their families had come from elsewhere? Did they somehow neglect to realize that if they went back no more than two or three generations, every single one of them would find their families roosted comfortably overseas somewhere?

"You know what?" Ava said, eyeing them and noticing that the vast majority of the group were men. "Let's split up for this. I'll play the role of cop and you go in there, the big and burly man that you are, and see if you can identify with them. Sort of a spy."

"That does sound like fun," he said. "You sure you can handle approaching that group, though?"

She gave him a playfully disappointed look, as if to say: *Are you kidding me right now?*

He held up his hands in mock defeat. "You're right. Sorry."

"Me first," she said and started over towards the group. The closer she got to them, the more she started to understand why Frank had asked if she could handle it. None of the men looked particularly threatening; in fact, most of them looked fairly scrawny. But the anger in their faces told a different story. She liked to think that anyone trying to prove a point in a civil manner wouldn't get physical with a detective but then again, she was finding that the concept of a *female* cop was a bit too much for some to handle.

She approached the group as timidly as she could, not wanting to alarm anyone. She took a proper count of them and saw that there were eleven people altogether—nine men and two women. One of the women looked like she did not want to be there, probably ordered to come by her husband. There was no chanting of any kind, but Ava supposed that was because it seemed to have just gotten started. But there was plenty of conversation, and none of it was especially kind or positive.

She honed in on one man in particular that was speaking a little louder than everyone else. He had the rapt attention of three others in the group, nodding along with everything he was saying.

"...and they're starting to worm their way further into the city," this man was saying. "It's not enough that they're stealing up a lot of the good jobs down at the docks but now they want more. And no one on the city council or government seems to give a damn!"

"We need to kick them all out," one of the listeners said. "Toss every single one of them on a boat and send them back to wherever they came from!"

It was more than Ava could stand. If she heard much more, she wasn't sure she'd be able to keep a civil tongue. "Excuse me," she said. She had her badge at the ready but did not flash it like a shield. She simply held it out for the men to see. All four of the men in front of her did a double-take. One of them even smiled and looked to the men next to him, as if making sure they weren't being pranked.

"A lady dick?" one of the listeners said. "You the one I've read about in the papers?"

"Might be," Ava said. "You fellas aren't out here trying to start trouble, are you?"

"No," said the man that had been griping about the loss of jobs. "We're assembling peacefully in a public setting. We're doing nothing wrong." He snickered and took a quick look at her chest. He then stepped forward and said, "You care to join us?"

"Not especially. I just find it curious that you're choosing to hold your protest *here*, so close to where the immigrants live. If you want people that matter to hear your message, shouldn't you be in a more influential part of the city?"

As the men let this sink in, Ava noted that one of the women was looking at her as if she was wearing a suit of armor and carrying a fabled sword. A woman detective may be a laughing matter of no real importance to men, but she was proud that most women saw her feats and accomplishments as a beacon of opportunity.

The apparent leader of the little group, the one she'd originally heard speaking, gave her a challenging look. "If we're not disturbing anyone, why's it matter where we do it?"

Unflinching, Ava said, "It just seems to me that your gathering here is just so that the immigrants can hear how much you hate them. It has nothing to do with actually wanting change."

The leader sneered at her but when Ava did not remove herself from his presence, the men that had been listening so attentively to him stepped away slowly. She wasn't sure if they sensed trouble on the air or if they just didn't like being in the presence of a policeman, but they were clearly uncomfortable.

Somewhere else from within the crowd, she heard a whispered voice that irritated her even further. "This city would be so much better if police like her just went through and arrested all of them."

"*Killed* all of them is more like it," came the hushed reply.

Ava didn't bother turning to see who'd said it. She kept her gaze on the leader. He took his eyes away from her slowly and held up his wooden sign. It had been created using a piece of old plywood and a fragmented two-by-four. It contained a rather simple message, written in harsh brush strokes. **IMMIGRANTS GO HOME.**

"Immigrants aren't welcome in New York City!" he bellowed to the other side of the street, seemingly to no one in particular. Ava supposed the protest was more about the spectacle than anything else. There were people over there, walking by and going about their day, but they seemed to ignore the small group of protesters for the most part.

As she looked around to see if there was any reaction at all, she spotted Frank quickly approaching. He gave her a quick wink as she made her way out of the crowd. Not wanting to seem too obvious, she remained at the side of the group, as if standing there to make sure the protests didn't get out of hand.

As Frank weaved his way into the crowd and started playing his part, Ava once again looked to the anger in the face of the leader—the same sort of anger and resentment that was present in the faces of the others in the group (with the exception of the clearly out-of-place wife). The idea that Eve's killer might be among them didn't seem very far-fetched, but an even more alarming feeling came over her as she considered it: if this one group was so filled with hatred toward immigrants, how many others in the vast and growing city felt the same?

CHAPTER NINE

Frank decided to step on it when he saw Ava and the apparent leader of the group get a little too close. He knew that Ava could completely hold her own in a fight, but he'd much rather it didn't come to that. He hurried over towards the group but by the time he got there, things seemed to have diffused a bit. The leader had started screaming his nonsense out into the streets, but at least he and Ava were no longer having their little staring contest.

He felt slightly relieved when he passed by Ava. From here on out, the bulk of the attention would be on him if he did his job well. He'd been truthful with Ava in the car. He understood the grievance these people had but thought they were a little too vocal and not going about finding a solution the right way at all. At the end of the day, he knew they were all really immigrants. His own family had only come to America from Italy about ninety years ago, his grandfather settling somewhere down near Virginia in the early 1800s as a young man with a pregnant wife and just a bit of money. He'd never met his grandfather but had heard stories about him. And if his grandfather had been an immigrant, he didn't see how the notion of coming to another country with the hope of starting a new life and a new trajectory for your family was something to be torn apart.

It was a notion that made it harder than he thought to get into character—not that he was that great of an actor in the first place. He did his best to seem like he wasn't quite sure if he should be there or not, figuring that going all-in might draw too much attention to himself. A few of the men in the group saw him coming in and moved to let him join them. He approached a man near the back of the group and gave him an uncertain smile. It was a good thing he wasn't in his traditional dick uniform today. Having no active case to work on, he'd come to the office in casual garb. Before Ava had planted them on this case, he'd had a long day of sitting around the precinct to look forward to, waiting to see what calls might come in. As it turned out, dressing like an everyday joe was going to come in handy.

"So what's going on here?" Frank asked. "Did something happen?"

"No. Just trying to get the message out."

"Trying to enlighten people on the problems all these immigrants are causing?" Frank asked.

"Exactly."

"Mind if I join?"

"Absolutely not!"

He looked over to the other side of the group, where Ava made a slow retreat back to the car. As far as he could tell, everyone in the group had pretty much forgotten her. Their voices started crying out to anyone on the streets that would listen, screaming simple yet hateful phrases. He couldn't feel any real tension in the air, but Frank knew all too well how quickly these co-called peaceful demonstrations could get out of hand. He'd never been *inside* of one, so he did his best to keep his police instincts at the front with his newfound acting ability.

"There's no room for immigrants in these streets!"

"It's hard enough for local folks to get jobs!"

"Get back on the boat, you freeloaders!"

Like Ava before him, he noted that there were no immigrants on the other side of the street to hear these phrases. However, he did know that the immigrant neighborhoods started just about two blocks to the east. They had been smart in their planning; by not standing directly in the midst of the people they were accosting, they stood less of a chance of getting into trouble. It made him think that this might not be the group they were looking for. If Eve Buzek's killer was part of a group like this, he doubted such a group would take such safe precautions.

Still, he didn't see the point in wasting the opportunity. If he had this bunch of boobs this close and easily swayed, it shouldn't be a problem to get some information out of them.

He looked back over to the man he'd been speaking to a few seconds ago and nudged him. "You having trouble looking for work?"

"Nah, man, not me. I've got a pretty good job down on the docks on the night shift. But the amount of these crooks coming down trying to get jobs…it's disgusting. You want to see good, hard-working people losing work because of these scumbags, just look at the factories and cleaning companies. Immigrants coming and working for dirt cheap. I don't blame the business owners for going that route because it saves them money, but…damn if it isn't scary to think of what it's gonna be like in a year or so."

"For sure."

"How about you?" the man asked. They'd also attracted the attention of two others that were listening in over the din of chants, shouts, and roaring complaints from the rest of the crowd. "Have they taken anything from you?"

It was eerie how quickly he came up with an answer. Maybe he was a better actor then he thought. "Just my peace of mind."

"I hear that." The man, eager to make friends and acquaintances that shared his barbed beliefs, leaned in closer. When he spoke again, he did so quietly, in a whisper of conspiracy. "I tell you what. I consider myself a Christian man, but these immigrants trying to come in here and steal our jobs and property." He shook his head in disgust. "If I ever got the chance to blow one down…"

He left the comment unfinished, as if the first half of the sentence spoke for itself.

Sensing his opening, Frank nodded sympathetically. "Oh, I know. I know." He let the comment hang, taking a look around at the rest of the group. In the time he'd joined them, they'd taken on two more members. One of them carried a sign that read **NO FOREIGNERS!**

"Hey," Frank said, leaning in close to his new, fake friend. "You guys ever do anything other than this? Anything a little more…hands on?"

"Nah, man," the fake friend said with a disappointed frown. "It's just too risky. It's not worth risking your future for, you know?"

"I suppose," Frank said, rolling his eyes. "But I've heard stories, you know. Stories about some really determined citizens that are putting a real scare into immigrants."

"Oh, I have, too. There's a small group right in the heart of that dump all the immigrants live in. One of the guys used to work with me."

"Are you serious? What sort of things is he doing?"

The man seemed to hesitate for a moment before shaking his head. "I don't think I should say. Please understand…I don't know you from Adam. I can't be risking that sort of thing. I'm not trying to get anyone into any trouble."

Frank knew he was very close to overstepping, so he did his best to pull it back. More than that, being in the presence of these people was irritating him. He wasn't sure how much longer he could stand in the center of their vitriol without losing his cool.

"I respect that. But do you think you could maybe point me in that right direction?"

Again, the man didn't seem too sure. But at the same moment, the leader of the group started shouting one of his simple and hateful phrases. It seemed to give the man a bit of courage, a spark of encouragement to assist this apparently like-minded individual.

"A few days ago, this guy came to us and talked about forming a mob in the street—running down through those shitty buildings they're all living in and breaking some windows, pushing some folks around. Nothing too deadly, just enough to cause a stir, maybe draw some blood, you know?"

"You know his name?"

"No, and I don't think he ever gave it. But he did tell us where to meet him."

Frank pretended to think it over and even manage to place a small smile on his face. "And where might that be?"

The man seemed delighted to be able to provide this information and when he leaned in closer to Frank, a stranger might have thought they'd been close friends for a very long time. "I'll tell you, but you'll want to be careful when you leave here and go looking for him." He nodded to the right, in the direction of Ava as she continued to assess the scene from afar. "That lady is a cop and was snooping around just a little while ago. And between you and me, a dame with a badge and gun makes about as much as sense as these immigrants trying to waltz in here like they own the place."

Frank had to grit his teeth a bit before he answered. "I'll be careful." And then, smiling towards Ava and hoping she saw it, he added: "And I think I can handle a lady cop, anyway."

They both laughed at the comment, but as the man gave Frank the location, Frank found himself having to fight the urge to punch the man in his face.

CHAPTER TEN

"A butcher shop?" Ava asked. "That's what he told you?"

"That's exactly what he told me. And there was one man that overheard it and he seemed to get a little uneasy."

"Well, it's worth checking out, I guess. It's not like we have any other leads."

This started to feel abundantly true as Frank drove the car two blocks out of the way, just to get around the protest and to stay out of sight of the people they'd both just spoken with. She felt their little stop by the protest had been worthwhile, but it was a little maddening to feel like they were essentially chasing ghosts. While the tip that had singled out a specific butcher's shop was a good one, she also knew that hoping to find just one single person that held a grudge against immigrants in this part of town had the potential to be very difficult.

Ava wasn't especially familiar with this part of town, so when Frank parked in front of the butcher's shop on the other side of the street, she had to reorient herself. "The alley where Eve Buzek was killed is just a few blocks over that way, right?" she asked, nodding to the west.

"Right. So someone living or working so close would be familiar with the area."

They shared a look that spurred Ava on, giving her reason to hope that a notable clue or a next direction would be waiting for them in the butcher's shop. She got her first real look at the place as they crossed the road to it. A simple sign over the door read Baker's Butchers and Meats. A single, large picture window showed the interior of the shop; both the glass and the inside of the place looked grimy.

Frank took the lead, opening the door. The smell of fresh meat was overpowering but not in a negative way. If anything, it made Ava want a steak—a delicacy she hadn't enjoyed in over six months or so. The place seemed to be empty of customers, and there appeared to only be one employee working. A large man with massive shoulders stood behind a low counter. He was working at a large section of beef on a well-worn chopping block. A white apron hung from his waist, stained with blood and numerous, unidentified wet spots.

43

He turned to them as they approached the counter and gave them a genuine smile. "Howdy folks. Give me a second, would you?"

He continued carving off a section of beef from the larger chunk. He used a cleaver to do it, working with it the same way an artist might use a brush. Ava had never seen someone use a cleaver or knife with such efficiency and, as odd as it seemed, beauty. The fact that the man was quite massive made it all the more notable. When he was done with his current cut, he buried the cleaver into the remaining chunk of meet. Turning to meet his visitors, he wiped his hands on the front of the apron.

"What can I do for you folks today?" he asked.

"Is this your shop?" Frank asked.

"It is. Name's Chester Baker. The shop belongs to me and my brother." He gave them a curious look and tilted his head. "Not from this part of town?"

"We're not, actually," Ava said.

"In fact," Frank added, stepping closer to the counter. "We were hoping to ask you some questions." That said, he produced his badge from the inner pocket of his coat. Ava wasn't sure why, but she rather enjoyed watching him do it.

Chester Baker took a small step back at the sight of Frank's badge but then folded his arms over his chest. It wasn't necessarily a defiant move, but it was a non-verbal way of letting them know their badges didn't scare him.

"Questions about what?"

"Well, we were just chatting with a small group of protestors about five blocks away from here. Seems there's a rapidly growing hatred towards immigrants, especially in this part of the city. Tell me, Mr. Baker, have you ever participated in one of these protests."

"Yes, I have. Several of them. But that's not a crime, is it?"

"Not at all," Ava said. "In fact, I daresay it's one of the things that makes this nation so great and alluring to people from other countries. This *city,* in particular."

"Yeah, sure. Cops have to say that sort of thing, right? Look…I'm not exactly busy here, but I do have some work to do. So if—"

"Yes, the questions," Frank said, interrupting. "Mr. Baker, have you ever resorted to violence during any of the protests you've taken part in?"

"Not a single time."

"Have you ever gotten confrontational with anyone?"

Baker nearly answered this but then let out a chuckle that had absolutely no humor in it. "Did some pigeon give you my name?"

Frank looked to Ava, and she read something in his eyes that she'd seen before. She wasn't quite sure what he was trying to communicate, so she did her best to read the situation. Chester Baker was a beast of a man, and he was clearly not all that intimidated by their presence. She wondered if Frank had picked up on this, too. And if he had, was he going to delve back into his surprisingly full bag of acting tricks? Maybe the almost mischievous look in his eyes was his way of saying: *Just follow my lead.*

"Mr. Baker, you seem to misunderstand. You said you thought that as police, we have to take a very specific stance on the immigrant issue. And for the public and the newshawks, you're absolutely right. But as people that live in and love this city…well, that's a different matter altogether."

Baker looked confused but remained unmoving. Ava thought he might sense a trap and was unwilling to say anything else; he wanted them to show more of their hand before he opened his mouth again.

"Why do you think they hired me?" Ava asked. "One of the things the police have always wanted was a safe, relatable face—something to show the public that the police are not just a group of hardened men looking to arrest people for trying to find a drink somewhere or being in the wrong part of the city at the wrong time. With the Women's Bureau, the force has a nice, clean face. It's a distraction, though, because yes…while we have to take the stance that we are pro-immigration, hardly anyone on the force likes it."

Frank wasted no time. He walked closer to the counter and then looked toward the front door, as if making sure no one else was about to come inside the shop. "The group we just spoke to told us we could find you here. Between the three of us and that slab of beef over there, this immigrant situation is going to start cracking at the foundations in another few weeks. So we're looking for people that are a little more dedicated than others. People that might be willing to go an extra mile when the time comes. This is more than just the two of us," he said, playing a hand on Ava's shoulders. "This is deep in the department. And if we hope to make change on this issue, it's going to have to be quiet. And that's why we're looking for people on the streets to sort of keep tabs on the temperature of things. Do you understand what I'm trying to say?"

Baker was grinning now, but he still had a suspicious look on his face. "You expect me to buy this? I'm not a simp."

"This isn't something we can come out and *ask* you," Ava said. "Let's be honest here, I'm sure you've heard about the cops that are working closely with the mob on certain things. This is no different. And I can give you an example. Just yesterday, an immigrant woman was killed in an alley right beside the tenement building where she was living. Now, we have to look into it and file a report. Right now, it's not that big of a deal because *we* were assigned the case. But if detectives that are sympathetic to immigrants had gotten the case, there would be trouble. They'd be grilling protests groups, coming to men like you that are rumored to be a little more aggressive that most. However, what I can tell you right now is that if you or anyone you know was involved in that girl's death, you may need to just lay low for a few days."

She could see the slow evolution of relief in his eyes. Baker's posture relaxed a bit and by the time she was done, he, too, was looking out of the picture window to make sure no one was about to come inside.

"So, you...you can help me to know when it is safe to go on marches? To make sure we won't be interfered with if we do decide to do a little bit more than protest or march?"

"Yes. But you need to help us, too," Frank said. Ava wasn't all that surprised that they had managed to get on the same wavelength so quickly. "We have to file some sort of report on this dead girl to keep our captain happy. Can you tell us *anything* at all? Did you even hear about it?"

"Oh, I heard about it. Anytime an immigrant dies around here, it's a small victory. But I heard that this one might have actually been murdered. Which, if you ask my opinion, is even better."

Ava thought of poor Eve Buzek—who had never done anything ill or hateful toward another human being—naked and dead on the coroner's table. The rage she then felt toward Baker welled up in her stomach like lava and she had to make sure not to let it show on her face or in the clenching and unclenching of her fists.

"Any clue who might have done it?"

"Sorry, no. I know a lot of people that would happily tell you they want to kill these roaches, but I don't know that they'd ever do it.

"Were you here, working all day yesterday?"

"Yes. All day."

"And if it came up in official questioning, you could prove it?"

"Yes, I believe so."

"Good, good," Frank said, sounding relieved and sympathetic.

"Look, detectives, we have a march planned for tomorrow night, just down the road a bit so they can see it from the tenements. Should tomorrow night be safe?"

Ava couldn't believe the luck they'd stepped into but took a moment to pretend as if she was thinking. "What time, exactly?"

"Eight at night."

She looked to Frank, almost enjoying the bit of playacting they were doing. "I think that should be fine. I'd just wrap it before nine, if possible."

Baker nodded gratefully. She didn't think he completely trusted them, but it was close. "We can be done by nine. And if not, we'll pack it up like good boys and girls and go back later. I don't believe I could ever kill another person, but it sure is nice to scare the hell out of them. Me and a buddy of mine had this one woman begging us not to hurt her one night. Offered to let us do anything we wanted with her. Almost took her up on it, too, but she—"

Damn, Ava thought as she felt herself snap. The charade she and Frank had worked to build up came crashing down in a single instant as she felt the boiling rage shoot through her entire body. She took two huge strides toward the counter and, not really thinking about it, took out her badge. She knew Frank had already done it, but in that moment it seemed necessary.

"You're one miserable son of a bitch," she said. "How dare you even joke about assault or abuse against a defenseless woman in such a way! How dare you—"

"What the hell is this?" Baker demanded. "Bunch of liars!"

"Better a liar than a—"

Frank took her by the arm and led her toward the door. She could feel some rage in his grip, likely from having to listen to the deplorable nonsense coming out of Baker's mouth. She fought him for just a moment, then gave up when she realized how quickly she'd snapped. They could have likely got much more information out of Baker if she hadn't flipped her lid. Once she understood the mistake she'd made, she allowed Frank to lead her back outside onto the street. She caught one last glimpse of Baker before the door closed behind them.

"Ava." That was all Frank said. That was all he needed to say.

"I know. That was stupid of me. But I just couldn't listen to it."

They both seemed to notice that he was holding her hand at the same time. They slowly removed themselves from one another and took a step back. "You have to remember; we're trying to catch a killer. Sometimes that means sitting in the nastiness of other people."

Ava typically did not like feel as if she was being spoken down to or like she was a child, but she knew in this case that she deserved it. "I know. I'm sorry."

"No, you don't need to apologize. It was just sort of a shock."

"We could have gotten more information out of him. Frank, really, that's my fault. I'm sorry."

"It's okay. We'll have another cop swing by here today and then make sure we have a few men out in this area to keep an eye out— make sure things don't get out of hand if there *is* another march planned like Baker said."

Ava nodded, willing herself to get over her mistake. They still had half the day to work on this. And the way she saw it, the tenement neighborhoods were so thick with people that surely someone knew *something*. Plus, there was something else…something Baker had said that may have been more helpful that she'd realized at first.

"The way he talked, did you get the impression that immigrants are harassed more than we're hearing about?" she asked.

"Maybe. And really, it wouldn't surprise me. I think even the immigrants know it's a waste of time to report any crimes against them."

"So I think we should ask around. Maybe even forget seeking answers strictly about Eve for right now. If we can look into reports of bullying, abuse or even murder, maybe that will provide us with a trail that will lead back to Eve."

"But maybe not here in this neighborhood," Frank said. "We saw this morning at Eve's place that no one is exactly excited about talking to the police."

"That's why we go back to the station. We'll look at other reports that were made. The way I see it, if an immigrant thought something was worth reporting, it had to be pretty bad and with considerable details."

"If the cops that took the report down were worth a damn," Frank pointed out. "But yeah, I think it's a good place to start."

They headed for the edge of the sidewalk to cross the street back to the car. Just before they did, Ava looked back through the large picture window into Baker's Butchers and Meats. She saw Chester Baker back at work on his slab of beef, only this time there was nothing delicate about the way he worked. Instead, he was working on the meat as if he were trying to kill the animal all over again.

CHAPTER ELEVEN

When he wants, he can be as quiet as a ghost. He's gotten quite good at blending in and not drawing attention to himself. He did it as a boy, when many of these piss-soaked streets were nothing more than etched dirt trails meandering closer to the city proper. While his father was robbing people and finding a new, faster way to get drunk, he was learning to move along without being seen—picking pockets, stealing food, getting peeks of women servicing men just like his father through the grimy windows of seedy back-alley parlors.

By the age of twelve, he'd watched these women at work, he'd seen fist fights break out over poker games, and he'd even seen a man bleed to death after a dispute over a three-dollar debt ended in a knife to the throat. And though he came to know and love the secret, dirty lives that were played out in those dusty alleys, he always came back to a little perch in the alley behind what his father had often called a cat house. Others called it a parlor, a whore house, and a variety of other things.

He'd watched the women flirt, peeked at them through windows, and even watched one get raped in a fit of rage right outside the door. He lost his virginity to one of those women at the age of fourteen. She'd been hesitant because of his age but when he showed her the money in his pocket—stolen from a game of poker the night before where every participant got so piss-drunk that they passed out—she stopped refusing. He'd gone back to that same woman countless times and fell in love.

Later, she'd died of a bad heart, and he went on with his life. Now, at the age of fifty-one, he was starting to understand how messed up it was that she was the only woman he'd ever slept with. Oh, he'd propositioned women here and there but had always been rejected. He'd paid women of the night for their company but had never been able to perform; he'd always allowed them to keep the money so long as they held him until he fell asleep.

But now that part of him had stirred awake and realized how broken it was. Even as a child, he'd understood how vile and wrong the act of rape was. Watching the scene in the alley all those years ago had aroused him, sure, but he'd also been stricken with a certainty: rape was the lowest thing a man could do, even lower than murder as far as he was concerned.

He felt the need to be with a woman. It had never left him, and he had done his best to nurture it by returning to those alleys, hiding away for most of his thirties and forties as the city grew up and became this whole different thing all around him. And each time he watched a man exchange his money for the woman's time and company, something inside of him dwindled away and he knew that if he was to ever feel that satisfaction again, it could not be with a woman that he paid. Perhaps that was why he'd always failed to make love with them after his first love had died. Maybe deep down he knew he wanted something more.

He thought he'd found it with Eve. He'd met her three weeks ago and had even helped her put her clothesline back up after one of the ends had frayed and come undone form the post along the side of her neighboring building. They'd talked about many things that day—about where she was from, what she hoped to do here in America, and her feelings on New York. And then when he met her outside her building one night like they'd agreed, he'd tried to kiss her. She had denied him, and he'd felt something come dislodged inside of him.

He'd killed her two days later. It had been easy, and he knew right away that if he had to, he could do it again. It got him to thinking, that was for sure. In this city, no one that mattered gave a damn about immigrants—especially immigrant women. If he kept pursuing them and had to kill them, no one would know. Besides, he'd tried enough local women. And apparently, he was not to the liking of anyone. There had, on one occasion, been a middle-aged woman that had taken him out behind a speakeasy and done her best to coax him into action and it had *almost* happened. He'd been so frustrated that she had nearly been his first victim. But his embarrassment of not being able to perform had crippled him as she'd gone back into the building, laughing and already seeking out her next possibility.

He was so very glad she had not been the first woman he'd killed. She'd been too eager for him. Hell, she would have serviced anyone. No, he wanted something special. He wanted to feel wanted by someone that was *un*wanted. He thought if he could somehow arrange that sort of situation, it might fix whatever it was that was broken inside of him.

It had not worked with Eve, but through her, he found that he could kill and that was almost as satisfying as sex…based on what he could remember of the act, anyway.

Eve was dead now and her body had been moved. The cops seemed to not really care. They'd stayed for maybe ten minutes and Eve Buzek was just another dead immigrant. One less problem for the city to worry about.

But now there was someone else. He didn't have time to look too closely because he had to go back to work. But he watched her easily, spying on her like a ghost as she made her way through the street vendors along the side of the street. From what he could tell, she was looking for a pair of shoes. Even he could see that the bottoms of her current shoes were worn out, her heel sticking out of the bottom and touching the pavement. He could see it from where he hid behind a newsstand just twelve feet away from her. She knew him, but not well. She certainly had no idea that he was following her and already thinking of how he might try to entice her to sleep with him.

At this point, though, thinking of Eve, he'd be fine if she said no. He'd kill her, too. One way or the other, he'd have his satisfaction.

He watched this new girl, so frail and pretty and lost in a city that might very well swallow her whole. He smiled, studying the curve of her neck, the small lumps of her breasts beneath her ratty shirt, her nimble legs. Yes, given time, this city and its blackened heart would swallow her alive.

Maybe he'd be doing her a favor by killing her before the city did.

CHAPTER TWELVE

When they arrived back at the precinct, Ava felt the need to hurry. She even felt that if they could get in and out without Minard spotting them, that would be even better. Here they were, less than five hours into trying to solve the case and they were right back where they had started—the safe confines of the precinct.

They split up almost right away, Frank angling to the right of the reception desk to head for the Records room. Ava decided it might be a smarter play to check with the Women's Bureau. After all, the majority of immigrant cases weren't handled all that seriously and given only the bare minimum of effort. Therefore, she figured the majority of them ended up on Frances's desk.

She hurried downstairs to the WB offices and was surprised to find every work desk empty—with the exception of Frances. She was sitting at her desk, looking over a stack of paperwork and eating a sandwich without much interest. She glanced up at Ava and gave a confused smile.

"Back already?"

"Yeah. Where is everyone?"

"Out to lunch. I stayed behind to make sure this paperwork is finished up on time. I'm starting to feel a lot more like a secretary than a policewoman, I'll tell you that much. Is there anything I can do for you?"

"Maybe. I only learned about this Eve Buzek case because you and Lottie mentioned it this morning. It made me wonder how many other immigrant cases come through here, hardly anything at all to report, that end up on your desk."

"Oh, we get a few here and there. Lottie was even assigned to one a few weeks back, but it came to nothing."

"A murder case?"

"No. Just a fight of some kind. An immigrant man ended up with a deep gash on his right forearm. If you're looking for murder cases regarding immigrants, I'm afraid you aren't going to find much. I know they're hated by a lot of people out there, but I don't know that it's come to actual *killing* just yet. With the exception of Eve, of course."

"If I wanted to find records related to the cases like Lottie had, where would I start?"

"Well, you don't need to look back any more than a year. No one started taking crimes against immigrants seriously at all until then." She paused here and opened the bottom drawer of her desk. Ava heard her rifling through a few folders and papers, eventually coming out with two sheets of paper and handing them to Ava.

"What's this?"

"These are cases that have been sent down to the WB that involve abuse, harassment, or minor fights. As you know," Frances said, giving a mocking tone, "us pretty little ladies aren't equipped enough to handle much of anything else. But if you're looking for cases like the one Lottie dealt with recently—with immigrants being put under any sort of threat—it's listed here. That should help you find them much easier up in Records. But let me warn you—there's likely not much. Most undocumented immigrants aren't likely to file reports with the police."

"This is fantastic, Frances. Thank you!"

Frances nodded, returning to her sandwich. Ava couldn't help but notice the chagrined look on her face. Or maybe it was a resigned sort of jealousy; she had to sit down here dealing with paperwork while Ava was out with Frank, tackling real issues and real cases. Ava couldn't help but feel a bit sad for her as she left the WB offices and returned upstairs.

She found Frank still in the Records room. He was standing over the long table in the center of the room with a few folders scattered out in front of him.

"Anything?" Ava asked.

"Maybe just one thing for far. What reads like an attempted kidnapping of a fifteen-year-old immigrant girl a few months ago. The parents were able to fend the attacker off, though. You find anything downstairs?"

She placed Frances's two sheets on the desk. "Just a way to save a hell of a lot of digging."

They scoured the Records using the shortcut Frances had provided. Out of fifty-one entries, it seemed that only eleven involved immigrants. And thanks to the list, the entire hunt only took them forty minutes.

Of the eleven reports, two were so sparse in their details they were essentially useless. Out of the other nine, six involved life-threatening situations. And it was out of these that Ava came across a report that seemed to echo Eve's case. The report, which was from just two months ago, told a very basic account of a young immigrant woman named Wanda who had narrowly avoided being murdered. The report was so sparse that there was not even a last name given. However, it was listed that Wanda indicated she had come from Poland and had only been in New York for three weeks before the incident occurred. Though she'd managed to escape the encounter with her life, she'd suffered a few broken fingers and multiple lacerations on her face. In the report, Wanda said the man came at her with a length of rope, springing from a hiding spot in an alley. The address given for the woman was on the same street Eve Buzek lived on, just about seven or eight blocks further south. The attack itself apparently occurred on Ellis Island. The final note on the report was that Wanda was terrified when she was questioned and made little sense.

Irritated with the lackluster effort put into the report, Ava slid it over to Frank. "I think this might be a decent place to start—the address given as place of residence. And the sad thing is that if you and I hadn't been looking for something exactly like this, I think it's safe to say it would have been buried. I can't see where any follow-up work was done."

Frank read over the file, starting to nod slowly as he came to the end of it. "Yeah, I think the address makes it worth looking into."

"The length of rope the man was carrying is what has me thinking we're on to something. I mean, what might he do with a length of rope other than strangle her? Just like Eve was strangled."

"So we have half of a name and a potential address," Frank said.

"And only about half a day to get an answer," Ava pointed out. "I don't see Minard giving us another day if we don't have anything close to a lead by the end of the day."

Frank nodded his agreement and said, "We'd better get moving then."

***

It was almost dizzying to head back to the Lower East Side for a third time in less than six hours. As far as Ava was concerned, it was almost a sign; to get any kind of answers and solve this case, they were going to have to spend a great deal of time here. If there was a killer out there using the alleys and nooks and crannies of the tenements to their advantage, he knew the area well. Perhaps she and Frank were going to have to get to know the area, too.

They arrived at the address the report had indicated. It was yet another pair of buildings that were nearly stacked on top of one another, allowing just a thin space between. Like the other alley they'd visited that morning, it was filled with clotheslines and garbage cans. While there were no young ladies currently working on laundry, Ava did spot a sickly-looking feral cat gnawing on a rat's corpse. It seemed to add to the filthy atmosphere, highlighted by a mess just to the right of the cat that she took to be human excrement.

The building on the left side of the alley looked to have been condemned. The windows had boards over them, and there were chains and padlocks across the door. On one of the boards covering the windows, someone had painted two words: GO HOME. It was a simple two-story building and the upper portion just before the roof took over seemed to be crumbling. She wasn't sure how long ago the building had been tossed up, but she would be very surprised if it remained standing of its own accord after another year or so.

The building on the right seemed to be perfectly fine, though. In the shadow of its rejected neighbor, it looked almost normal. A simple concrete stoop sat in front of a well-worn wooden door. There were no windows along the front but as Ava and Frank approached the door, they could hear all manner of speaking inside, including a young boy's high-pitched laughter.

Ava knocked on the door and almost right away, the voices inside stopped. As they died down, Ava was certain she'd counted at least seven different people. She heard the faint shuffle of footsteps coming towards the door before it was finally opened. The door opened up only a crack. The man looking out had bags under his weary eyes. His hair was wild and all over the place, and a growth of haggard beard covered most of his face.

"Yeah?" the man said. "Can I help you?"

"I hope so," Ava said, sensing Frank angling in behind her in a protective position. "We're looking for a woman named Wanda that is supposed to live around here. I don't have a last name, just that she was—"

"Are you cops?" the man interrupted.

"Detectives."

The man's eyed widened a bit as he shook his head. "No. I have nothing to say."

"But we're looking for—"

"I don't know a woman by that name. Sorry."

When he closed the door on them, Ava nearly started to knock again but lowered her hand at the last minute. She looked to Frank, and she could see the frustration in his face. "Have the police really been so negligent of these people that they don't trust us?" she asked.

"Seems that way, doesn't it? Although, I think they're not willing to speak to us out of fear. It's almost like they're afraid we've come just to flush out the illegals and that's all."

Ava stepped down off of the stoop and walked to the next building. There was no alley between them. It was basically just one building, divided by a difference in the tone and texture of wood and very sketchy gutter system that ran down the front of the building.

"I get their hesitation and all," Frank said as they approached the next door, "but we *are* cops. We don't always just have to smile and nod when someone closes a door in our face."

"You take this one, then," she said. "I don't know that I could be hostile towards these people."

Frank took the lead, stepping to the door and knocking. The sound of his large fist against the puny door sounded no different than as if Frank had knocked on the side of a hollow carboard box. More voices could be heard in this building, but they didn't bother keeping quiet when the door was answered like their neighbors had. The door was opened seconds later by a woman of thirty or so. She held a small bowl in one hand, and a baby on her hip with the other. The baby was gnawing on one of its fingers, a thick river of drool running down its plump arm.

"Yes?" the woman said.

"Sorry to bother you, ma'am," Frank said, "but we were wondering if you know a woman named Wanda that lives around here."

"Wanda?"

"Yes. I don't have a last name, but we do know she ran into a bit of trouble recently and we'd like to have a word with her."

Ava could see the realization start to bloom in the woman's eyes. She backed away from the door, looking to the floor. The baby stared out to the detectives, very interested in the visitors. His saliva-caked arms were filthy, as were the bottoms of his feet.

"Ma'am, we're only here to help," Frank said. "Another woman was found dead recently. And she lived close to here. We're just trying to figure out why."

This did not affect the woman at all. She closed the door in their faces. The baby made a few little noises behind it as Frank raised his hand to knock again. Before his fist connected, though, the door opened. This time, there was a man dressed in overalls and a tee shirt standing there. Ava assumed this was the husband. Although, to make that assumption in a neighborhood where some single dwellings housed as many as ten or twelve, it might be a very faulty assumption.

"A woman died, you say?" The man had a very thick accent that was unmistakably Irish. He was rail thin, and Ava couldn't help but wonder when he'd last had a proper meal. She supposed if he *was* the husband, most of that family's nourishment was going to the baby.

"Yes," Frank said. "Just right down the street a ways. Less than a mile from here. A young woman that came from Poland."

Ava saw the look of anger cross the man's face. He placed his hands on his hips in a defeated posture and looked out onto the streets. "We wondered when someone was going to just stop pretending and go ahead and start killing us."

"What do you mean?" Ava asked.

"Are you the police?"

"Yes, sir."

"Why have you done nothing about the harassment? Sometimes I see two or three of you at once and though your presence here does keep some of the recklessness at bay, you leave as if you can't stand to be here."

"Maybe be careful how you use the word *you,*" Ava said. "I'm sure as hell not clustered in with that sort, and neither is my partner. As he said, we're here because a woman has been killed and we'd like to speak with another woman named Wanda that was attacked a few weeks ago." She pointed down to the thin alley and added: "She lived just down there, less than fifty feet from where we're standing."

"Yes, I know. We knew Wanda quite well. She helped take care of William, our boy."

"You *knew* her?" Ava asked. "But not anymore?

"After she was attacked, she left. She was staying in that condemned building with a few others. A few days after her attack, she left....which was a shame because she'd only been here for a week or so. I think she might have had some issues with her papers; they were trying to tell her she was still considered illegal, I think. She was very private about it all."

"Do you know where she went?"

He leaned against the doorframe and gave them a skeptical glance. "She's in no trouble?" he asked. "I have your word?"

"Yes, you have my word," Frank said. "We truly only want to help."

"She got away from here. She and three other women she was living with managed to get an actual apartment. It's in what she called the Garment District. They all got jobs working for a seamstress. You can probably find her there."

It was clear that he felt guilty for giving them the information, but Ava thought she could see a glimmer of hope in his previously skeptical eyes.

"Thank you," Ava said. "We'll make sure she doesn't know it was you that told us where to find her. But you have our word: we're only wanting to ask her questions to hopefully find this other woman's killer."

The man nodded and shrugged all in one motion. Apparently, he didn't care one way or the other. She hated that people in his position had grown accustomed to not trusting anyone, used to being lied to and overlooked. It helped her to realize that was actually one of the reasons she so badly wanted to find Eve Buzek's killer. Eve, like so many of the immigrants in this city, had gotten used to being overlooked.

By solving the murder, maybe it might make up for it in a small way. Maybe in solving the mystery behind Eve's death, Ava could help the thousands of other worried immigrants feel like they were finally being seen. She knew it would only be a small step, but it was a necessary one—and one that Ava was more than happy to take.

CHAPTER THIRTEEN

It was called The Garment District for good reason: the number of clothing shops seemed to grow every month and, ever since the terrible fire at the Triangle Shirtwaist Factory in 1911 where one hundred and fifty people died, most of the shops were reputable. Ava knew about the fire because she recalled Clarence talking to some friends about it one night over a poker game. One of his elder friends had nearly broken down in tears as he'd recalled the failed attempt to free some of the workers.

Ava wasn't sure where that old building had once been, but she caught herself looking for it as she and Frank made their way down the streets, They'd parked the car a bit farther back, figuring it would save a lot of time to walk and check on each shop. Because of the sheer number of seamstresses and clothing shops, Ava feared it might be hard to locate the correct one.

As it turned out, though, Frank's deep well of detective instincts saved them quite a bit of time. They'd been walking for roughly ten minutes, having passed three clothing stores and one seamstress's shop, when he stopped and nodded to the opposite side of the road. He was nodding to a small shopfront without any sort of signage out front. The only indication it was a seamstress outfit was because of a hand-made sign on the other side of the glass. It read: *Seamstresses and material haulers wanted! ALL welcome to apply.*

"I bet that's the place," he said. "No sign for the business and so badly in need of help that it's the only clear indication of what the building even is. Also, if you look through the window, the main part of the shop is dark."

"Okay...?" She was beginning to enjoy these little moments where Frank had clearly noticed something before her but did not simply want to give her the answer. He wanted her to figure it out, to enhance her own skills as a detective. So, instead of waiting for him to give her the answer, she went with her own train of reason. "And if the main floor is dark, that means the work is being done deeper in the building, maybe even in a basement—where anyone just strolling down the street can't look inside to see the sort of people that are working there."

"Good job," Frank said, giving her a playful clap on the back. "Now, let's go see if we're right."

They crossed the street and, though the front area of the shop was indeed dark, the front door opened to them quite easily. It reminded Ava of how the laundry had been set up when they'd gone looking for answers about Eve's employment. Standing in the front room, they could hear murmured voices coming from elsewhere in the building. Ava thought she could also hear a chorus of clicks and hums from what she assumed were sewing machines.

"Hello?" she called out.

After a pregnant pause, she finally got a response. "Oh, hello!" a male voice called out from behind a wall on the other side of the front room. "One moment, please."

Ava and Frank waited, Ava again being reminded of the laundry. It was clear that the helpful woman back at the laundry had been doing her best to keep the immigrant workers out of sight of passersby on the street. The same was apparently true here as well.

After another minute or so, a man in a shirt and basic pants came out to greet them. His shirt was drenched in sweat and his hair was just as soaked, but he looked to be in a mostly good mood. "Something I can do for you?" he asked.

Frank showed his badge, and the man didn't seem to even bristle at the sight of it. "Detectives Wimbly and Gold, with the NYPD. We're looking for a woman that we are told is working somewhere in the Garment District. Her name is Wanda."

"Got a last name?" the man asked.

"No. But *is* there a Wanda working here?"

"Oh, I've got two Wandas. One is roughly forty or so, and the other just turned twenty-two the other day. Say…has either of them done something wrong? As far as I know, they're both here legally."

"No one is in trouble," Ava assured him. "The Wanda we're looking for was involved in an assault three weeks ago. The way we understand it, she barely escaped with her life."

"Ah, then that would be the twenty-two-year-old Wanda. Wanda Polanski. She's…well, she doesn't really like talking about it; I tried, and…no offense. But she doesn't think highly of the police, with how it was all handled."

"We're here to remedy that," Ava said. "Could we please have a word with her?"

"Of course. Stay here and I'll get her."

The man left, leaving Ava feeling surprisingly positive about him and the operation he was running here. Had they actually stumbled across a business owner that cared about his immigrant workers? The mere fact that he knew Wanda wasn't keen to talk about what had happened to her showed effort and consideration on his part. For Wanda's sake—and the sake of the other immigrant women working under him—Ava hoped that was the case.

It took another three minutes before a young woman came around the corner in the back. She was short, quite thin, and looked like a scared animal. Her blonde hair hung down tightly to the sides of her face. Even before she was standing in front of them Ava could see some scarring on her chin and cheek. She supposed these could have been remnants of the attack she'd survived.

"Wanda?" Ava asked.

The woman would barely even look up at them, though she did seem surprised and somewhat relieved that there was another woman there. In one of their unspoken communications, this all pointed toward Frank taking a back seat on this interview, letting Ava run with it.

The young woman nodded, giving Ava the briefest of glances. "Mr. Milner says you needed to ask me questions."

"That's right," Ava said. "First, I think maybe I should apologize on behalf of the entire police department for not following up on the case you filed. We'd like to ask you some more questions about what happened to you. We're under the impression that there may be a man taking the lives of immigrants. A young woman was killed just yesterday, not too far away from where you used to live. My hope is that some of what you can tell us can help us find him. Would that be okay with you?"

"Yes. If I can help…"

Ava gave her a few moments to collect herself before she asked her first question. "All we know if that it occurred on Ellis Island and that the man came after you with a rope. Is that correct?"

"Mostly. I was waiting for a boat, and it had just gotten dark. A man came up to me and when I knew he was focused on me, I tried moving away. He said he thought I was pretty and wanted to show me a good time. Dinner. Maybe some dancing. I told him no and he seemed to take it well. But then he came back a bit later…"

"How much later?"

"Maybe five minutes. And I didn't even know he was there until it was too late. He said something about…something…"

Wanda stopped here and lowered her head. Though her hair did a good enough job of hiding her face, she also used her hands to keep their gaze away from her. It made Ava think she was more than just scared to bring up the memory, but maybe embarrassed or ashamed as well.

"It's okay," Ava said. "We're only trying to help here. I do have to tell you, though, that we don't have much time."

Wanda nodded, tucked her hair behind her ear and tried to go on. "He said something about making sure he'd make it feel good for me and then there was something around my neck. A piece of rope, like the kind they sometimes use to tie crates down with. He was strangling me, but he was also…he was also rubbing himself against me from behind. I thought he was going to have me right there…and I think he might have…"

She started to cry, but it was only tears dripping from the corners of her eyes. She took a deep breath and managed to get herself under control.

"I don't know if he would have killed me first and *then* had his way with me or the other way around. I just don't know…and I keep wondering even though I was freed."

"How *did* you get away?" Frank asked.

"There was another woman there, an older lady. She saw it happening and yelled at him. She was Russian, I think. Screaming at him and yelling for help. It scared him away and when he yanked the rope away, it tore my face up a bit, as you can see. Also, when he first started trying to strangle me, I snapped two of my fingers in trying to loosen it."

She held up her right hand and showed them where her pinky and ring finger had been taped together with sturdy, white medical tape.

"Did you by any chance see your attacker's face?" Ava asked.

"Just from the side for a moment when he first came up to me. But he came off as being just too confident, too *forward*, so that I looked away."

"Is there anything else you can think of that might help us? Anything that seemed strange to you?"

Wanda nodded and Ava watched a fear slowly descended on her again. "When he asked me to dinner and dancing, he called me by name. *'Hey there, pretty little Wanda.'* That's what he said. He knew my name."

"So it was someone you know?"

"I know it sounds daffy, but no. I had only been here for a few weeks at that point, and I knew very few men. And the men I *do* know are all smaller." She grinned nervously here and added: "And they're all immigrants. They all have accents. But this man was very much an American, I believe. No accent, and he was quite strong. I could feel it in the rope around my neck and the way he pressed into me."

"You're certain of this?" Frank asked.

"Of course I'm not certain. I never saw his full face. But I just knew…in the way he said my name and the violence I felt from him. This was no one I knew. He was a complete stranger, but he knew my name."

With this, Wanda spilled a few more tears. Ava looked to Frank, concerned and now feeling that this went deeper than either of them had suspected. Her mind was already flooded with new questions and possibilities—and they all rode the tide of Wanda's harrowing last comment.

"He was a complete stranger, but he knew my name."

CHAPTER FOURTEEN

Despite having lived in New York City her entire life, Ava had never stepped foot on Ellis Island She had, of course, heard about it but had heard differing opinions of the place. What surprise her the most when she and Frank stepped off of the ferry and onto land was that it was not nearly as crowded as she'd expected. She knew that over the last few years it had become a place known more for the deportation of illegal immigrants than a place where new immigrants were processed—and yet somehow most of the public seemed to overlook this fact and choose to be angry about immigrants in general.

"You know," Frank said as they walked along a sidewalk that led to a large concrete and brick building in the center of the island. "A lot of folks refer to this place as the Island of Tears."

"That's…awful. Why?"

"Because so many immigrant families are broken apart here. Some are allowed to stay in the country while others have to leave."

There were countless comments that came to Ava's mind, but she kept them to herself. As they came to the building—which Ava assumed was some sort of processing center—a man in a well-pressed police uniform checked their IDs and badges before allowing them inside. Beyond the front doors, they entered into a large room that was currently occupied by three single file lines that were all inching closer to a long counter near the front of the building. Things were mostly quiet and there was on overall feeling of defeat hanging in the air. This was not a place where people went to feel hopeful. As time dragged on and the purpose of the island evolved, it seemed to be less about the hope of starting a new life and more about facing the laws and defeats that ruined them.

Wasting little time, Frank avoided the lines altogether and walked to the far side of the room where an armed police officer was standing as a sentry of sorts. Ava tried to imagine what it must be like to stand here all day in the event that some angry immigrant being threatened with deportation started to get violent.

When they approached this officer, he seemed delighted to have the company. He smiled warmly to both of them even before they were standing in front of him.

"I take it you work security here?" Frank asked.

"I do. You two are cops?" He turned what sounded like a basic comment into more of a question as he eyed Ava.

"We are," Frank said, showing his badge. "Detectives Wimbly and Gold."

"Gold? As in *Ava* Gold?"

"That's her alright," Frank said, knowing that Ava hated just about everything about the burgeoning notoriety around her name. She wasn't quite a city-wide name yet, but the newspapers during her first few weeks on the force had sure made an effort to make that happen. She had to constantly remind herself of that whenever she was on a case, keeping herself in check when it was time to make a quick decision.

"Oh, wow, it's a pleasure to meet you," the security guard said.

"Thank you," she said, hating the fact that she was pretty close to blushing.

"Tell me something," Frank said. "You see much action around here?"

The guard gave a shrug of his shoulders and looked around as if to say: *You see this, right?* "Not much. But you do see a lot of interesting characters."

"We're looking into a murder, and we think the killer may have tried striking her a few weeks back," Ava said. "There was a young woman that was attacked three weeks ago, sometime at night. You hear anything about that?"

"Can't say that I did. But then again, my shifts are over at five. So if it happened after that, I wouldn't have been involved anyway."

"But you didn't hear rumors or gossip about it?" Frank asked.

"No. Was it an immigrant?"

"It was."

"Well, there you go. An immigrant being attacked isn't going to really hit the grapevine, now is it?"

As Ava tried to think of how to answer this, there was a slight commotion behind them, coming from the front of one of the lines. A man had started speaking very loudly provoking murmurs of unrest and excitement from those around him. Ava watched as the guard they'd been speaking to reached for the baton strapped to his left side.

"But I've done everything I've been asked to do!" the man at the front of the line was screaming. "If you do this, what will become of my wife and son?"

The answer went unheard over the growing din of whispers from within the other lines. But the man's response to whatever the answer might have been was again loud.

"No! That's not right! You can't..." he stopped here, as if he'd only then realized how loud he was being. He then leaned in closer to the man behind the counter that he'd been speaking to and resumed a normal volume.

As things settled down, Ava realized she'd been just as tense as the guard. The three of them shared an uneasy glance and then Frank picked things back up, as smooth as ever. "Have you *ever* heard stories about immigrants being attacked here on the island?"

The guard thought it over for a moment before shaking his head. "Can't say that I have. But there are fights *between* the immigrants every now and then. Nothing bad, just enough to make 'em jingle-brained."

"Do you think we might get some different answers if we speak to the clerks and other officers that work here?"

"It's doubtful. As far as I know, everyone sort of keeps to themselves. Even if there are some stirrings of trouble, we keep out of it. Immigrant business is not our business, you know?"

Ava thought it might have been the most ignorant thing she'd heard all day. Of course, she said no such thing. Fortunately, the guard had a sudden thought, speaking up again and making sure she didn't have time to say anything.

"But you know...there was a bruno that worked here. One of those behind-the-counter guys that had to make sure all the forms were filled, and all the tests were done. He'd lose his temper real easy and even chase some of the folks out. I had to get on him about that a few times. He was a real hard-ass; you know the type? Thought he was in charge of the whole show. He got fired for poor conduct but would come back every now and then just to stir things up. He always left after a single warning, though."

"What do you mean by *stir things up?*" Ava asked.

"Trying to make sure no one here was taking it too easy on questionable immigrants. Threatening to have any deported if they so much as complained a single bit about anything. It may sound mean of me to say so, but I was glad when they fired him. And even happier still when he stopped coming by."

"And how long ago was that?" Ava asked. "When was the last time he showed up?"

"And when was he fired?" Frank added.

"They cut him loose about….let's see, maybe five months ago? After that he'd pop up maybe once a month or so, like he was *looking* to cause problems. But it's been a while since I've seen him or even heard about him showing up."

"Would you say it's been over a month?"

"Oh, yeah. Easily. Maybe as much as two months."

"And what's this fellow's name?" Frank asked.

"Harvey Jackson. Do you think you'll pay him a visit?"

"It's likely," Ava said. "Thanks for your help."

"Oh, for sure. Good luck with Harvey, by the way."

"Why do you think we'd need it?"

"Harvey always spoke highly of cops," he said. "But he complained all the time about how the cops aren't hard enough on illegals. And, no offense, Mrs. Gold, he was furious when he found out a woman had been promoted to detective."

Ava couldn't help but smile. "Well, then, I can't wait to meet him."

CHAPTER FIFTEEN

They were able to get Harvey's Jackson's address from the payroll department and, as if they needed any other indicators that they were on the right track, it turned out that he lived less than ten minutes from where Wanda had previously lived.

"Well, it would almost make sense, you know?" Ava said. "By working on Ellis Island and having access to records, he could easily find out the name of a woman he took a liking to. Also, the timeline syncs up."

"How so?" Frank asked, driving back toward the tenements yet again.

"If he was let go about three months ago and kept making appearances up until a month ago, that would have given him plenty of time to stalk and study his victims. And that lends more credibility to the pre-meditated murder approach."

Frank considered it all as he came to an intersection and stopped to let a horse-drawn carriage pass. Ava watched it with a degree of great interest, wondering how much longer horse-drawn travel would be a normal sight in the city. It seemed like things were evolving at such a fast rate—the city growing by leaps and bounds almost overnight it sometimes seemed—that such sights would be a thing of the past sooner rather than later.

They arrived at Harvey Jackson's address just minutes later. While it was fairly close to the run-down part of town they'd been focused on so much throughout the day, it was a rather nice building. The exterior actually reminded Ava a bit of her own apartment building. It was yet another reminder of how quickly the city could change on you; just a few blocks could mean the difference between a well-to-do neighborhood and one where you could never be too certain about your safety.

Jackson lived on the ground floor, in the apartment all the way down the main hallway. Being just shy of two in the afternoon, Ava wasn't expecting much but they had to try. If nothing else, they could revisit the place later in the afternoon. Yet, after Frank knocked on the door, it was answered in just a few moments They did not see Harvey Jackson on the other side, though. Instead, there was a middle-aged woman that looked as if she'd been caught in the middle of baking something. Her apron and the sleeves of her dress were powdered in flour.

"Yes? Can I help you?"

Ava noticed that when Frank spoke, he was reaching for his badge but seemed to decide not to pull it out at the last minute. "Yes, ma'am, so sorry to bother you," he said, slipping come charm into his voice. "I was hoping to have a word with Harvey. Is he in?"

"No, I'm afraid not." The woman looked confused but not alarmed, which Ava thought was a good sign. Then again, there was something a bit off about the confusion. She seemed genuinely surprised that anyone that might know Harvey would know he would not be home.

"You're his wife, correct?" Frank said.

"That I am."

"Would you mind telling me where Harvey is?"

"He's at work."

"Oh, I see. Do you mind telling me where he works?"

The slightest bit of alarm showed up in Mrs. Jackson's eyes. "I'm sorry, but who are you?"

It was then that Frank showed his badge. "I'm Detective Wimbly, and this is my partner, Detective Gold. We believe Mr. Jackson may be quite helpful in answering some questions we have about a recent crime in the area."

"Oh…oh, I see. Is he in some sort of trouble?"

Apparently, Frank had not yet fully stepped out of his acting role from earlier. What came out of his mouth next sounded far too natural to be a lie. "No, no, of course not. No, we believe he may know someone that we're looking for."

Ava watched relief flash through the wife's eyes. A smile touched her mouth, followed by the faintest traces of a frown. "Well, that doesn't surprise me. Working down on Ellis Island with all those disgusting immigrants, he'd be bound to see a crime or two. Especially now that they've got him going out and sniffing around those deplorable immigrant neighborhoods."

It was a stark enough statement for Ava to have to keep her facial expressions in check. *My God,* she thought. *This poor woman has no idea her husband lost his job three months ago. So that begs the question: what's he been doing during these past three months when he left the house, his poor wife not knowing any better?*

"Yes, ma'am," Franks said. "I'm sure you understand that we can't tell you any of the specifics about the crime itself, but…well, you pretty much hit the nail on the head. I wonder, though…do you know where he might be? Which neighborhood he was sent to today?"

"No, sorry. He doesn't really tell me *where* he's going. But I do know that it's not very far away. He tells me how he walks to and from these neighborhoods, right from our front door."

Ava wasn't sure why, but there was something in the way she said this that made her think the wife might have some sort of suspicion that something was amiss. Maybe she did know that her husband had potentially lost his job and was choosing not to tell her. And, being a subservient wife, she wasn't about to confront him on it. Maybe when finances got in a pinch, but not now.

"That'll be tough," Ava said, also slipping back into acting mode. "With no criminal history, Mr. Jackson has no files at the precinct. We've only ever gotten his name. We have no idea what he looks like. Can you give us a quick description? You've seen those neighborhoods, I'm sure—packed so full of people it's hard to tell one from another."

The wife sneered and nodded her head. "Oh, don't I know it. It makes me scared for him most of the time. But he shouldn't be too hard to find. He'll probably be the only one not dressed in rags and reeking of shit. I believe he was wearing his black overcoat when he left this morning. And his bowler hat. He has a well-trimmed black moustache. Is that good enough?"

"Yes, ma'am, I believe it is," Frank said. "Thank you so much for your help."

Ava couldn't help but notice that the wife wore a grin of satisfaction on her face. In her eyes, not only had she been able to help the police, but her husband may be a man of some importance in whatever case they were working on. Ava couldn't help but feel a bit bad for her, considering her husband had been lying to her about his job for the last three months.

***

Because they were pressed for time, it made more sense to search for the man from the car; they'd cover a lot more ground and save a ton of time. However, searching for one lone man on the crowded streets in the immigrant neighborhoods from a moving car was going to be incredibly difficult. When they pulled over and decided to canvass the streets on foot, Ava could basically feel the minutes ticking away.

The one thing they did have going in their favor, though, was that it was still well before five in the afternoon. A great many of the men in the neighborhood would likely be out trying to find employment or the next meal for their family.

After just a few minutes of searching, the task started to seem out of their reach. Ava figured they needed to take any chances they could, even if that meant asking questions of an immigrant population that had clearly decided the police were not on their side. She approached a man in a tattered suit, holding tightly to the hand of his much younger and very thin wife. Like Frank had back at the Jackson residence, Ava decided not to pull out her badge. In this particular situation, she figured it might do more harm than good.

"Excuse me," she said as they approached the couple. "I was wondering if you might be able to help us. We're looking for a gentleman by the name of Harvey Jackson. He's likely well-dressed, has a noticeable bowler hat and, we suspect, may be trying to cause a bit of trouble."

The man eyed them was a great deal of skepticism, and Ava wondered if there was just something about her that was now coming off as a little too demanding. She'd always told Clarence that she could usually spot a cop even when they weren't in uniform, and she wondered if she was now that kind of not-so-subtle cop.

"Sorry, no," the man said in a clearly Irish accent. And then, already turning his back to them, he added: "We've seen no one like that."

Frank seemed to be biting back a remark as they hurried past the couple. "We're going to probably get that sort of treatment a lot," he said.

"I figured as much."

"We need to isolate the areas we think someone looking for specific immigrants might be. Maybe some place that is freely helping them find employment, or a cheap pub."

A thought occurred to Ava, one she was rather embarrassed for not thinking of right away. "Or the same sort of place where Eve Buzek was killed."

"The alleys," Frank said. The look on his face suggested he felt a little foolish for not thinking of it first.

Ava took the lead, and they weaved their way through the crowds. She started in the direction of the tenement buildings, thinking that the killer had chosen the alleyways running between the immigrant homes for the sake of convenience. There would certainly be a smaller chance of witnesses, and the police would have not been quite as hard pressed to arrive on the scene. So if they were truly dealing with a killer that was targeting immigrants, those alleys would be the prime location to do it.

It took two blocks of walking before they came to the first of the residential buildings. Like most of the others they'd seen today, it looked about one or two steps away from being condemned. They came to the first alley and found it empty, not even adorned with the clotheslines they'd spotted so many times. There were small piles of trash here and there but nothing else of note.

They slipped past that alleyway and came to another one. Here, there were two young boys playing a very simple game with a broken wooden crate and a stick. When they saw the two detectives peering down at them, they stood upright and pretended to not be playing their destructive little game.

Taking a shot, Frank took a few steps into the alley. "Hey there, boys. I'd like to ask you a few questions if—"

The boys turned around and ran away. One of them laughed nervously as they came to the end of the alleyway and took right where the alley came to a T-intersection with another. It was the first alley they'd seen today that intersected at all and Ava knew that's where they needed to go. If there was a legitimate network of alleys that ran beside and behind all of these buildings, that's where they needed to look. Ava did her best not to focus too much on the fact that there would be several blocks to check. If they struck out completely with their alley search, they'd easily waste the remainder of their day.

But it made the most sense and the lack of argument from Frank showed that he agreed. They started down the alleyway and Ava was surprised at just how on edge it made her feel. There was nothing inherently dangerous about the alleys, but the tight space and the uncertainty of what waited for them around the next corner caused her to instantly put her guard up. She slowed a bit to let Frank take the lead, not realizing she'd done it until he squeezed past her.

At the T-intersection the boys had taken, they followed in their footsteps, heading off to the right. The boys were long gone, leaving this alley just as empty as the one before it. This one did boast two clotheslines and a makeshift sawhorse where someone looked to be repairing a door The craftsman was nowhere to be seen, though.

Halfway down this alley, they came to the opening to another alleyway on the left. It ran down between two nearly identical buildings. This one looked more like what they'd been seeing all day: a network of clotheslines, a few people loitering about, piles of trash here and there. Frank headed in that direction, presumably to see if he could ask questions of the four people at the other end of the alleyway.

But before they could get there, an alarming sound grabbed their attention. It was coming from just ahead, to the left where yet another alleyway opened up. It was the sound of a panicked man, not quite frightened but certainly distressed, followed by the jostling of something metallic. With just a brief glance exchanged between them, Ava and Frank went running in that direction. Frank got there first, coming to a skid as he made the turn into the new alleyway. Ava came in just behind him and had just enough time to see what was happening before things started to happen very quickly.

A man in a rather nice suit and a bowler hat had pinned a frail-looking man wearing a stained shirt and dingy pants against one of the tenement walls. In the scuffle, they'd knocked over a trash can. The well-dressed man was cocking his arm back in a fist.

"Show me your papers or I'm going to knock your teeth down your throat!" the man in the hat yelled.

"Police!" Frank yelled, darting forward.

Almost unbelievably, the man in the bowler hat—who did indeed fit the description the wife of Harvey Jackson had given then—looked as if he was going deliver the punch anyway. But he dropped his arm at the last minute as Frank went rushing at him. He grabbed the man by the lapel of his shirt and pressed him against the wall face-first.

"What is this?" the man Ava assumed to be Harvey Jackson demanded. "I'm only doing my job!"

"Are you Harvey Jackson?" Frank asked.

"I am!"

"Last we heard, you don't have a job." Frank expertly cuffed him as Ava approached the immigrant. He had a shiner just below his left eye, no doubt delivered by Harvey Jackson.

"I was only making sure he wasn't here illegally!"

"Even if he wasn't, that's not your place," Ava called out.

"What's the m—are you cuffing me? Get me outta these bracelets! I was only doing my part to keep this country in order."

"That's fine," Frank said. "You can tell us all about it at the station."

"The st—now wait a minute…"

But Ava started to drown Harvey Jackson out as she noticed the looked of confusion and sorrow in the immigrant man's eyes. He had, after all, not done anything to deserve the accusations and beatings of Jackson.

"Sir, are you okay?"

It looked as if he were about to nod his head in the affirmative but at the last second, he shook his head. "I thank you for your help, but no…no, I'm not okay. None of this is okay. There are far too many men like that in this city."

"I know, sir. And we're trying to fix that."

"Seems you might be the only ones." With that, the man turned around and walked away, heading back out into the street.

And even though they now officially had a strong suspect in custody, the man's closing remark made it something of a bittersweet victory. They had a likely suspect in custody and that was at least one step towards correcting things.

CHAPTER SIXTEEN

Ava and Frank garnered a bit of attention as they walked through the front doors of the precinct together. She thought she saw a few looks of awe, while others simply rolled their eyes at the successful pairing. That was fine with Ava; as far as she was concerned, she'd love for the sight of her and Frank entering the building with a suspect in custody to become a very familiar sight to the group of men that had doubted her from the very start.

Being a slow day for the precinct, it didn't take any time at all for them to get Harvey Jackson into an interrogation room. When he was sitting behind the small table, his hands still cuffed in his lap, he remained indignant. He simply could not believe that an upstanding man like himself had been arrested for trying to make sure the city was not overcrowded with illegal immigrants.

"I'm not interested in who has the moral high ground here," Ava said as she and Frank stood in front of the table. "And while it's very sad that you find it necessary to go around beating up defenseless and hungry people, you should know that we didn't bring you in for that. Well—not only that."

"She's right," Frank said. "We'd been looking for you for about half an hour or so when we came across you in the alley."

"Looking for me? For what?"

"We're investigating the murder of a female immigrant," Ava said. "She was murdered yesterday, not very far away from where we ran across you today."

"And you thought I might know who did it?" he asked, clearly confused.

"Or that you did it yourself."

She saw the panic and absolute terror fill his eyes. He started to stand up but then seemed to think better of it and remained seated behind the table.

"Before you start prattling off again, let us explain," Frank said. "We started following a trail of sorts that led us out to Ellis Island, where a woman was attacked several nights ago. While there, we learned about you and why you lost your job."

"We were also told that you showed up several times even after you were fired," Ava said. "Just to scream and yell at people that had done absolutely nothing to you. And then today, we found you assaulting a man in an alley out in the tenements—not only close by where an immigrant was murdered yesterday, but *also* after learning that you've been lying to your wife about what you do all day."

"Does she still think you work on Ellis Isle?" Frank asked.

It was apparent that Jackson did not want to answer this, but the fear was still in his eyes. Now that he'd been told why he was there, he seemed to be a little more agreeable.

"Yeah. Yeah, she does. And because I always handled the finances and we had a bit saved away, she doesn't know any different."

"How *are* you spending your days as of late?" Ava asked.

"In a roundabout way, I *am* still working. Just not getting paid for it. I'm still doing my part to make sure this city isn't overrun by illegal immigrants."

"And that's what worries us," Ava said. "You just admitted to essentially trying to take things into your own hands. And now that we have a dead immigrant woman on our hands, you see how that looks for you, right?"

The reality of it dawned on him, and Ava could literally see his mood shift. He nodded and when he looked up to them, she saw a gentle sort of pleading in his eyes.

"I might be a mean bastard down deep and I do hate those illegals crowding up the streets." He gulped and then shook his head firmly "But as mean as I am, I ain't never killed anyone."

"This woman was murdered yesterday just shy of noon," Frank said. "Can you provide an alibi? Can you tell us where you were and if there is anyone that can back up your story?"

Again, Ava thought she already knew the answer when she saw the pleading in his eyes transition into relief. "Well, yeah. I was at a friend's apartment yesterday."

"At what time?" Ava asked.

"Almost the entire day. I got there just shy of ten or so and left around four."

"We're going to need the name of this friend and where he lives," Ava said.

"Fine, fine."

"And what, exactly did you and your friend do while you were there?"

"He's a buddy of mine that used to help at Ellis Isle—maintenance and clean up once or twice a week. He feels the same way I do. We sometimes get together and read a few different papers to see how the immigrant situation is being handled."

"And that's what you did all day yesterday?" Frank asked, skeptical.

"Yeah, honest to God. Played a few rounds of poker, had ham sandwiches for lunch." He again seemed to be overcome with a reminder of what his life had become. "I mean, I haven't told my wife about losing my job yet. So I have to find ways to fill my day. And yeah, sometimes I get a little rowdy when it comes to those immigrants, but I've *never* killed anyone."

"We'll check into your alibi and make sure you're telling the truth about that," Ava said. "As for now, though, we need to address the charges of you assaulting that man in the alley today."

"You serious?"

"I am. Very much so."

Jackson looked to Frank, saying nothing but giving him a look that seemed to translate into: *You gonna let this woman run things like this?*

Frank only shrugged. "Give me the name and address of the friend you were with yesterday, please. After that, we'll send someone in here to process you for the charge today."

"How long are we talking?" Jackson asked.

"A few hours," Frank said.

"Maybe even soon enough that your wife won't suspect anything. You should be home just in time for dinner."

Harvey Jackson looked at her as if he might strangle her if given the chance—his vow that he'd never killed anyone be damned. Ava ignored it and turned for the door as he gave Frank the friend's information. They had an alibi to check up on and though she was already pretty sure it was going to pan out, she tried to remain upbeat and positive. The day was coming to an end and so far, this was the closest they had come to any true lead.

There was a ticking clock and then there was the feeling of running out of time, and Ava was slipping dangerously close to the latter.

***

The friend's name was Lester Pinkerton, and he did indeed back up the story that Harvey Jackson had been with him for most of the previous day. The only hard proof he had was the crust of a ham sandwich in his trashcan and the confirmation that they did often spend their free time looking at the local papers about how the immigrant situation was being handled.

It was a wretched waste of time as far as Ava was concerned, yet there was something that Pinkerton asked them on the way out that made her feel uneasy—not about Harvey Jackson or Eve's death, but something else entirely.

"Hey, speaking of the newspapers," Lester said, his sad eyes trailing to the mess of pages on his kitchen table. "You guys think there's anything to all of this panic about money and finances? Is it going to get as bad as people think?"

Ava had no idea how to answer, so she was relieved when Frank did his best. "We're detectives, not financial experts. But honestly, I don't think it's much of anything to worry about just yet."

They left Lester Pinkerton with at least a bit of hope on the matter. When they exited his building, the first true signs of dusk were falling over the city. The streets were a little bit darker and filling up with traffic as people started heading home from work.

"So what now?" Ava asked as they got into the car.

"I don't think you're going to like my answer very much," Frank said.

"Let me guess. You want to call it a day."

"Well, that's what Minard gave us. And honestly…when the people that we're trying to actually help don't want to talk to us, it's sort of an uphill battle, don't you think?"

"Maybe…"

She hated the idea of giving up but, deeper down, she hated the idea of losing even more. She found it hard to believe that the entire day had somehow gotten away from them. Where had the time gone? Apparently, a string of failures and empty trails made the day go by quickly.

They arrived back at the station at 6:30, just shy of two hours after leaving Harvey Jackson in the interrogation room. Ava figured while he was still there and the day wasn't *technically* over, it wouldn't hurt to swing by the holding cell or office he was in and ask him a few more questions—questions that may lead nowhere, true, but she had to try. While Frank headed to his desk to finish up his day, she figured there was no harm in taking those few extra steps.

When she did not find him in the holding cells or at any desks in the bullpen, she grew confused. Had every single cop in this place totally disregarded Jackson and left him in the interrogation room by himself for over an hour? Sure, she thought he deserved such treatment at least for a little while, but there were protocols and rules to follow. She hurried to the interrogation room to process him herself but found the room empty.

As she stepped out of it and closed the door, she noticed one of the women from the front desk walking by, likely on her way out of the building to go home. It wasn't anyone Ava knew well, but she did know her name was Marie.

"Marie…the man that was here, in this room. Do you know if he was processed?"

Marie shrugged. "Not sure. I do know that some guy walked out of here about half an hour ago. Someone that was questioned earlier."

"Was his name Harvey Jackson?"

"I don't know. I'm just now on my way out. I can stop by the front desk to see. He would have had to sign out."

Ava did not like where this was going, and she somehow already knew what Marie was going to find for her. Still, she followed her to the front, where Marie slipped back behind her desk. She checked the visitor logs and nodded.

"Yeah, I have Harvey Jackson, departing about half an hour ago."

"What?" Ava said. "Who released him?"

A stern voice spoke up from behind her. "That would be me."

She turned and saw a policeman that she had seen countless times but had never bothered getting to know. He was one of the many that often greeted her with a roll of the eyes, a sneer of anger, or a quick glance down to the floor to avoid eye contact. She didn't even know his first name, only his last. She knew him as Hauser, a lumbering wall of a man. He was grinning at her, as if daring her to complain about releasing Jackson.

"Why'd you let him go?" she asked.

"Because he'd done nothing wrong."

"He was a suspect in a murder case we're working on."

"Right. He *was*. And let's be real here, sweetie. There's no way in hell he was going to be held or charged for assaulting an immigrant."

Ava surprised herself when she stepped toward him. His grin did not falter; if anything, it grew wider. "That was my suspect."

"And you left him here on other charges," Hauser said. "Flimsy charges at that."

"Is this supposed to scare me?" she asked. "The big man trying to step on the poor little woman's toes?"

This time, Hauser grinned so widely that his teeth showed. "It can be if you want."

Before she could say anything else, Frank was there. He had hurried over through a small crowd of other officers and employees that was watching the stand-off. He placed a gentle, reassuring hand on Ava's shoulder and led her away.

"It's okay, Ava. It's not worth it."

She let him lead her away, not back into the building, but toward the door. She saw Hauser still grinning, and a few others behind him watching on with great amusement.

When they were outside, with dusk continuing to darken the streets, Ava felt an uncharacteristic wave of shame passing through her. She wanted to cry, but she'd be damned if she'd allow it. Not because of men like Hauser. Not because of closed minds that still thought a woman couldn't possibly be expected to think for herself and make the right decisions.

"Ava, just take a breath, okay?"

She was barely aware that Frank had led her further down the street so that anyone looking from the stairs of the precinct wouldn't see her.

"This…this is never going to change, is it?" And in that moment, when the question came out of her mouth, she wasn't sure if she was referring to the immigrant situation or a woman's place in the workforce—especially in a workplace that was predominately male. And that made the entire situation even worse.

"I think it will," Frank said. "Eventually."

She thought of Eve Buzek, dead on the coroner's table, and of the faces of despair she'd seen in just about every immigrant they'd seen today. It fueled the anger in her but, at the same time, filled her with a sense of hopelessness that she felt far too deeply.

"Were you done inside?" Frank asked.

"Yeah. With Jackson gone…yeah, I'm done."

"Come on, then. With your permission, I think I'd like to walk you home."

Ava said nothing, only nodding. They walked side by side, further and further away from the precinct and she didn't even recognize when he slipped his hand into hers. She allowed it, even slightly squeezing back, as night fell upon the city.

CHAPTER SEVENTEEN

Ava checked her watched when they arrived in front of her apartment building. It was nearing eight o'clock, meaning Jeffrey would likely already be in bed. Her father was pretty lenient on rules, but even Jeffrey, at just eight years of age, had already learned to appreciate the value of a good night's sleep. She hated that she'd probably miss seeing him for the day but, selfishly, was also relieved that she may be able to simply relax on the couch and zone out.

"You okay now?" Frank asked.

"Yeah. I hate that Hauser got under my skin so easily."

"If it means anything to you, I think you handled it well. I'm not sure anyone other than Minard has ever stepped to him like that." He paused, waiting for a response. When he didn't get one, he gave her hand a squeeze. "Well, I've gotten you here. I'm going to head home, too."

She started for the steps, letting go of his hand, and turned back to him before she was fully aware of what she was doing.

"Do you want to come in for a bit? Maybe have some coffee?"

"It's not too late?"

"No. Jeffrey is probably already in bed. And even if he isn't I'm sure he'd be thrilled to see you again." With a playful frown, she added: "And Dad, too, I'm sure."

He smiled at her and joined her on the steps. "Then I'd love to. And I'll try to keep the boxing talk to a minimum."

As they entered, Ava realized it was the first time she'd even actually walked with him through the doors into the building. It felt surreal and she felt that familiar sting of guilt. The only man other than her father that had ever accompanied her inside the apartment building she called home had been Clarence. This had been their home, the first and only place they'd ever lived while married.

When they walked up the stairs and passed the first landing, she looked to the corner where, on one particularly cold January night, she and Clarence had kissed as if they were reckless teenagers, hands exploring and bodies heating up. And even as they climbed the stairs to the second floor, where her apartment and family waited, she could feel Clarence's ghost everywhere.

They didn't speak a word; Ava assumed Frank was also picking up on her slight tension. The silence remained between them until she unlocked the door and they stepped inside. She saw her father right away, sitting at the kitchen table and looking through the day's newspaper.

He saw Ava first but then his gaze drifted over to Frank as he came in behind her. Roosevelt's eyes grew wide for a second and it was clear that he wasn't sure how to handle the situation. Even though Frank had been over last night, that had been planned. Ava found it almost sweet that her caring father was still a little thrown off kilter whenever his daughter brought a man around.

"It's okay, Dad. I just asked him up for some coffee."

"Oh." He settled back into his previous position with the paper. "Need me to put it on?"

"I got it, if it's okay," Frank said. And, having been over the night before, he did just that. It made Ava feel oddly warm inside to see him navigating her kitchen with some familiarity.

Ava sat down at the table with her father, who was closing up the newspaper. "Is Jeffrey already asleep?" she asked.

"Yeah. He went out pretty quick. He played hard down at the gym today." He snickered here and added: "That kid is going to have one *mean* right hook."

"He's eight. Maybe we shouldn't encourage him just yet."

"You remember how young *you* were when you first stepped between those ropes?"

Her face started to get red as she said, "That's beside the point."

"How old?" Frank asked from the stove.

"You stay out of this," Ava snapped in a friendly manner.

"Five! And started working the bags at about six."

Frank laughed as he set the water to boil. "Oh, I can believe that."

Roosevelt understood when his moment to exit had come. He sighed, picked the newspaper up from the table, and got to his feet. He looked as if he might say something else but opted for silence as he gave them a friendly nod and left the room.

"He's okay with me being here, right?" Frank asked.

"Yeah. He won't come out and say it, but I think he's glad there's another man in my life."

"Did he take the loss of Clarence hard, too?"

His mention of Clarence rocked her a bit, but in a good way. Expressing the passing of her husband seemed natural, a surefire way to move on while also respecting him. "Yeah, I think so. But Dad never really expressed emotion very well, so I don't know for sure. Even if it *did* affect him, I don't know that he would tell me."

The water boiled and Frank finished up the coffee. He brought the mugs to the table and sat back down.

"We failed Eve Buzek," she said. "And I'm starting to feel like the entire force as a whole is failing that entire immigrant community."

"Our hands were tied," Frank said. "We can't help a community that isn't willing to talk to us."

"Have we given them any reason *to* talk to us?" But as soon as the question was out of her mouth, she shook her head. "Never mind. I just…I can't get over the fact that when we were there, out around that neighborhood, it was like I stepped into some other city. I hated that feeling. A feeling of division, you know?"

"We did our best."

He reached out and took her hand. "I think you managed to give at least a few people a little spark of hope—an inclination that maybe there *is* someone in power working for them."

"In power?" she asked mockingly. "Me?"

"Hell yes, you. You're an amazing detective, given that you never had any sort of training."

"I think working with you is training enough."

"That's good to hear," Frank responded. "A lot of the time, I feel like I'm slightly distracted."

"Distracted by what?"

He looked directly into her eyes, holding her gaze and her hand. "You. Seeing your determination and drive. Seeing the way you handle yourself and…"

He paused here as Ava began to slowly lean forward. She knew what she was doing and was slightly helpless to stop it. She'd wanted to kiss him for a while now but had felt the ghost of Clarence, just as she'd felt it coming up the stairway. But in that moment, looking into Frank's eyes, that ghost was fading. It was still there—it would always be there—but she could not feel it as strongly.

He leaned in to meet her, their mouths so close that there was an electric charge between them that she could feel in her breath. She closed her eyes, parted her lips and—

"Hey, Mommy!"

Jeffrey's voice may as well have been a bomb. She drew back, her heart leaping into her chest and a flush of red creeping into her cheeks. She wheeled around and saw her son standing in the kitchen doorway, still slightly squinting from having been stirred awake.

"Hey, sweetie," she said, opening her arms to him.

He came walking over and climbed up into her lap. "You doing okay?"

"Mmhmm." He glanced to Frank and raised a sleepy arm. "Hey, Mr. Frank!"

"Hey, kiddo. You still half asleep?"

"Nu-uh." He turned his attention back to Ava. "Thought I heard your voice."

"Well, I'm glad you came out. I don't like not being able to see you before I go to bed."

Despite Jeffrey's objection to Frank, it was clear that the kid was still partially asleep, perhaps roused by the familiar voice of his mother from another room. She hugged him and drew him close, holding him to her chest as she got to her feet.

She mouthed *"Be right back"* at Frank and carried Jeffrey through the kitchen and into the living room. As she carried him through the small living space, Roosevelt frowned from his place on the couch.

"I'm so sorry," he whispered.

"It's okay," she whispered right back.

She walked down the short hall, entered Jeffrey's dark room, and laid him back down on the bed. "G'night," she said, kissing him on the forehead.

Pretty much back asleep already, Jeffrey only gave a little *"hmmm"* noise in response. She looked down at him for a moment, wondering if he had any idea at all that there were a whole different group of people not too far away from where he slept comfortably—a group of people seeking the same safety and shelter he had while a great deal of the city turned their backs on them.

She left his room quietly and made her way back into the living room. Her father said nothing, just gave her an apologetic look from over the top of his newspaper. Ava shook her head at him, smiling, as she returned to the kitchen. When she got there, she saw Frank standing by the kitchen, sipping down the remainder of his coffee.

"He okay?" Frank asked.

"Yeah, he's fine."

Frank placed his now-empty cup into the sink and sighed. "Look...I'm trying to do what I feel is the right thing here. I think I should maybe go."

"Why?" She wasn't disappointed—not really. If anything, she admired his sense of moral right-and-wrong.

"What almost happened right there," he said, pointing to the table, "would have made me incredibly happy. But just last night, you expressed to me how you weren't quite ready for any of that. And even if you may have had a moment of weakness just now, I can't just let that happen. So I think I need to go."

His vulnerability made her want to kiss him even more, but she knew he was right. She walked over to him, placed a hand on his hip, and kissed him on the side of the face. "You're a good man, Frank Wimbly."

He grinned and headed for the door. "Yeah, let's keep that quiet for now."

She followed him to the door and watched him make his way down the hall. And as she watched him, she didn't feel Clarence's ghost within the hallway at all. Frank really was a good man, even though he often tried to convince others at the precinct that was not the case. It made her wonder how many hard-ass brunos down at the precinct might just be putting on a show for the other guys.

It made her wonder, too, how many people out among the marches and rallies against immigrants were just trying to fit in. Sure, she knew there were some bad apples out there, but she'd already seen today in the form of two business owners that there were some good people out there, too.

And while that did offer her some hope, she also had to accept the fact that there were others like their killer out there, too. And, just like those with hidden goodness in their hearts, she couldn't help but wonder how many of those were out there as well.

CHAPTER EIGHTEEN

It was easier to follow them at night, but it did take some of the thrill out of it. And deep down, he knew the thrill of being caught was part of the reason he did it.

He was getting tired, but that was nothing new. He hadn't been sleeping much these days. It took a great deal of time and effort to follow the women, to learn their schedule sand to know when to go after them. That's why he was currently sitting in the alley outside of a small textile warehouse. It was an area he knew well—perhaps better than anyone else in the city. He felt safe and even comfortable here, even knowing what he was about to do.

That comfort became something more like excitement when he heard the employee door around the back of the building open up. Being intimately familiar with the area, he knew that the light shrieking sound was one of the hinges along the edge of the door, badly in need of greasing. He heard the chatter of women's voices and the soft tread of feet on pavement.

There were four of them. And as soon as they came to the edge of the parking lot, they would splinter off from one another. Three would head east, and one would head north, towards that disgusting excuse for a neighborhood where all of the immigrants lived packed together like filthy rats. He knew all of this the same way he knew the way to his own home, the way he knew how to get to his own job. He'd watched and waited this long, so he knew her schedule like the back of his strong, flexing hand.

As the sounds of the four women faded away toward the back corner of the parking lot behind the textile warehouse, he slowly made his way to the back corner of the building. He saw their shapes, dark and standing out against the natural darkness of night. He watched them pause for a moment, talk, and then break off the same way they had every other night he'd studied them. The fact that his target was the one that always ended up walking by herself off to the north made it seem too easy.

He waited a few more seconds, not wanting to risk being seen by the other three as they headed out of sight. He then crossed the parking lot, sticking as close to the neighboring buildings as he could so that he would remain mostly hidden in night-shrouded shadow. When the quiet chatter of the other three women could no longer be heard, he took a left and headed north. He could see his target, small and looking very insignificant in the night. Her shape smudged against the darkness as she moved through the almost non-existent post-midnight foot traffic.

He saw one single figure pause to look at her. This filled him with an intense dread and jealousy. If it was a man trying to sweet-talk her or attempting to get her alone—well, that would not be ideal. Fortunately, though, the woman kept walking and did not stop. The man chuckled to himself and then carried on, apparently more interested in whatever task he was up to at such a late hour. He stumbled a bit and then sank down onto a stoop in front of a seedy-looking apartment building.

With the potential obstacle of a man out of the way, he was able to continue hunting. Although now, with her in his sights, it wasn't really hunting at all. The only thing left to do now was to take her.

He reached into to his right coat pocket and felt the scarf stuffed inside. He dried his sweaty hands on it, anticipating what was to come. He hurried his step a bit, still remaining as quiet as he could. She was a little over half a block away now and only had two more blocks to go before she would take a left and enter into that cramped hole she called home.

He drew closer, closer still…

And then she stopped. She looked to the right and waved.

For a moment, he thought she had spotted him and was waving him away in some odd, terrified way. But then he saw the other woman across the street. She was sitting on the steps of a closed shop, smoking a cigarette. The smoking woman stood, laughed softly, and waved his target over.

"Damn," he muttered.

Yes, he knew his methods were careless and reckless, but even he was not so foolish as to attack his target while another woman was there. Yes, he supposed he could kill both of them, but he had no idea if this other woman was an immigrant.

His blood boiled, and he clenched the scarf that had already strangled one woman tightly. He focused on the anger and tried to push it down. It was remarkably simple.

He'd watched her. She'd waited for this long. He could wait another day or so.

Besides, it wasn't as if these filthy immigrants were going anywhere anytime soon.

CHAPTER NINETEEN

Ava woke up with soreness in her neck and a haze over her mind. It felt like cobwebs had been spun in her brain the night before. She hadn't slept well, her mind overcharged with feelings of failure and worrying that Minard would not allow her and Frank another day on the Eve Buzek case. It was one thing to feel that she'd failed Eve; it was quite another to feel that she was also letting down an entire immigrant population.

She got out of bed slowly. She toyed with the idea of trying for another half an hour of sleep but knew it wouldn't come. Besides, she had a kid to help get ready for school. As usual, thoughts of Jeffrey lifted her spirits a bit, making it easier to get her day started.

When she made it to the kitchen, she saw that Jeffrey had already started eating his breakfast, usually the very last step before heading out of the door for school. He was eating a bowl of oatmeal with a piece of toast and jam.

"You make that yourself?" she asked.

Jeffrey nodded proudly. "I was going to make you some, but I didn't know if you even liked oatmeal."

"That's a sweet thought," she said. "Not a big fan of oatmeal. I think I'm going to cook up an egg, though. You want some?"

"Sure."

The following fifteen minutes had her feeling recharged despite her lack of sleep. Uninterrupted time with her son was like a magical elixir—one she wished she could get more of. She did her best to soak in every moment of it as they left the apartment and made the short walk to school. As usual she watched him walk up the sidewalk and through the double doors, not leaving until she saw him go inside.

She walked to the precinct with her mind torn in two different directions: first, thinking of Eve Buzek's case and secondly, wondering how last night might have shaped up if she and Frank had not been interrupted. She had no delusions that she would have invited him to her bedroom; it would be a long time before she crossed that line. But she also knew how much a simple kiss could change things between them. Even with the knowledge of mutual admiration and attraction, they were able to work cohesively together. But a kiss would likely turn all of that on its head…wouldn't it?

Surprisingly, the wondering stopped when she arrived at the precinct and saw him. She headed directly for his desk, noting the stares sent her way as she crossed the bullpen. Hauser was among them, and he looked just as steamed as he had yesterday afternoon. Ava ignored the stares (she was used to them by now, after all) and walked over to Frank's desk. He was already hard at work, typing something quickly into the beastly typewriter that sat on the edge of his desk. To her recollection, she'd only ever seen him use it once before.

"What are you working on?" she asked, propping her backside on the other edge of the desk.

He looked up and gave her a smile, a genuine one rather than a cursory greeting. "Figured I'd start the morning early. Try to get things going on a good foot. This," he said, tapping the paper rolled into the typewriter, "is my report for Harvey Jackson. I went back over all of the information regarding his alibi, put down some notes on Lester Pinkerton and all that. I wanted to get it down before I forgot it all since he was released so prematurely yesterday."

Ava had felt sure Jackson's alibi would check out, so she wasn't too disappointed over the news. The reminder of Hauser letting Jackson go, though, brought a new flash of resentment.

"Oh," Frank said, turning back to the report to finish it up. "I also caught Minard when I came into the precinct. I told him about some of the progress we made yesterday."

"You think that was progress?"

Frank only shrugged but offered her a brief smile—a smile she was coming to like a little too much. "Well, I had to make it smell good before he'd bite, you know? He seemed pleased and gave us today, too."

"That's great."

"Yeah, I thought so, too."

"Thanks for doing that," she said. And good Lord, there it was again—that desire to kiss him. Little by little, with every day that passed, he was starting to show her that he not only cared about his reputation around the precinct, but her opinion of him as well.

"I do need to tell you, though," Frank said, clacking away on the typewriter, "that he's said if anything else pops up or comes across his desk that needs our attention today, it's going to take priority over the Buzek case."

"Fair enough, I suppose. But really, while I'm glad to have the extra time, I feel like we're starting at the bottom again. All of our leads were dead ends and I have no idea where to start from here."

"Maybe that's a good thing," he said. He rolled the report out of the typewriter and placed it on his desk. "Starting from scratch lets us start from a new perspective. So maybe we do that, from the place we know we're most likely to find the answers."

"Back to the Lower East Side?"

"That's what I was thinking," he said, getting up from his chair and grabbing his coat from the back of it. Smiling at her and purposefully causing his hand to brush against hers, he said: "I'll drive."

***

It surprised Ava that the immigrant neighborhoods were really no different than the other parts of the city at this time of the morning. There was a good deal of foot traffic as many people either went out to work or continued hunting for jobs. It was a bit too early for any loiterers to be hanging around, which diminished the number of people to speak to.

Still, Ava found herself resorting to unfortunate stereotypes. Maybe, she thought, the immigrants that were either legal or possibly illegal and undocumented but understood the importance of finding work would be more willing to speak to them.

It was a theory that was put to the test within five minutes of Frank parking the car. Knowing that they stood a better chance of getting information if they didn't present themselves as detectives, they kept their badges tucked away. They also made the decision to leave their firearms in the car. The fewer clues to who they really were, the better.

They approached a man dressed in a blue work shirt, waiting to cross the street. He looked slightly lost and quite out of place. The nerves on his face only added to the sense of unease and Ava wasn't sure if she'd ever seen a more perfect illustration of a man on the verge of going to ask for a job.

Frank took the lead, as the rule of odds suggested most people in this part of the city would respond better to a man.

"Sir, excuse me, but I was wondering if you knew a woman named Eve Buzek."

"Buzek?" the man asked, thinking it over "No, I don't believe I do."

"Well, we were wondering if—"

"Sorry, but I really need to be going now."

90

Before Frank could say anything else, the man hurried across the street racing to avoid a man on a bicycle.

"More of the same, it seems," Frank said. "God, do I just *look* like a cop?"

"A little," Ava said, mostly joking. "But that's not a bad thing."

They took a few steps forward, about to cross the same intersection their failed interview had gone, when a sudden thought occurred to Ava. She halted, reached out, and took Frank's arm.

"Frank…the old woman that met us outside of the coroner's office. We should speak with her again. Maybe if she's on her home turf, she'll open up a bit more."

"True, but we have no idea where she lives."

"She said she lived close to Eve, right? I think we just start there."

Frank considered it and nodded after a few moments. "It makes sense, I suppose. This is crazy; as much time as we've been spending around there, we may as well move in."

Ava took a moment to get her bearings and turned to the left, the direction that would take them to the tenement where Eve had been living. It was only a few blocks away—not worth getting in the car and dealing with the traffic.

As they closed in on the building, it all started to feel a little too familiar to her. Maybe they *had* been here a bit too much in the past twenty-four hours. Ava looked at it as a good thing, though. What better way to get entrenched in Eve's life? What better way to understand what she had to live with and, perhaps, draw links to the person that killed her.

It seemed the streets grew grimier and more neglected with each step. The smell of sewage and garbage grew thicker with every few feet they walked. And before they knew it—almost as if the building had sprouted up from the ground ahead of them—there was the building Eve had lived in.

They had, of course, already interviewed some of the neighbors and had even gotten a bit of useful information from one of them. Rather that knock on those same doors again, they started at the end of the block. The first door they knocked on was not answered. Ava wondered if there was really no one home or if the residents were able to see the through the sizable crack between the doorframe and the door itself.

As they moved over to the next building, they passed by a thin alleyway that separated the dwellings. It was thinner than the one where Eve had died, little more than a small walkway where people deposited their trash. As they passed by, Ava saw a boy of about ten years of age, beating the dust from a tattered blanket against the wall.

Temporarily taking the lead from Frank, she paused at the mouth of the alley and entered. She took only two steps before the boy stopped what he was doing and looked at her.

"What are you up to?" Ava asked.

"Just I' this blanket clean."

"Which building do you live in?"

The boy pointed behind him. "That one. With my mom, dad, and three sisters."

"I don't suppose you have a grandmother that lives around here, do you?" Ava asked, taking one more step toward him. He seemed comfortable with her, and she hoped Frank's presence behind her wouldn't spook him.

"No, ma'am."

"Do you know of any older ladies that *do* live around here?"

"Oh, yeah," the boy said, smiling. "There's a woman next door, real old. Mrs. Maggie is what she makes me call her."

"Next door to *your* building?"

"Yeah."

"Thank you very much."

The boy nodded and smiled, a bit of red showing up in his cheeks. Ava stepped back out into the street and looked to the building beside the one the boy lived in. It was three buildings away from the one Eve had lived in—less than fifty feet from where Eve had been killed.

"You're way too good with kids," Frank said.

"It comes with being a mother," she joked, giving a cute little shrug.

Her eyes were already on the single concrete stair that sat in front of the door of the building where an old lady named Mrs. Maggie apparently lived. She lifted her hand and knocked, feeling the slightest stirring of positivity from the exchange with the young boy.

There was an answer at the door a few seconds later, though it did not open. An elderly voice called out from behind it, haggard and trying to sound tough.

"Yeah, who is it?"

"My name is Ava Gold, ma'am. I believe I might have spoken with you yesterday outside of the coroner's office. I was hoping I could have a few more words with you."

There was a very hushed "Oh" from the other side of the door. The silence that followed was almost long enough for Ava to knock again, but the old woman spoke again just as Ava raised her hand.

"I don't know…"

"Ma'am, we're just trying to help," Ava said. "We truly want to find who did this before he can do it to someone else."

There was an abbreviated silence again, but this time it was followed by the sound of a loud, metal lock unclasping from the inside. "Just get inside quickly," she said. "I don't want anyone knowing I was talking to you."

Ava didn't question it. She hurried in, looking back to make sure Frank was following her. She also took in the old woman's face and saw that it was indeed the same elderly woman that had greeted them outside of the coroner's office yesterday.

The interior was a bit more accommodating than the house Eve had lived in. There was an actual hallway of sorts, leading to a makeshift den. Beyond that, there appeared to be an open-walled room that served as a bedroom, but Ava did not get to see it. The woman, presumably Mrs. Maggie, did not invite them in beyond the front door.

"You still haven't found the killer, eh?" Maggie asked.

"No ma'am," Ava said. "And if I'm being honest with you, a lot of the people we're talking to aren't making it easy. I understand the distrust of the cops in this community, but when no one wants to give us any sort of information, it makes our job that much harder."

Maggie narrowed her eyes at Ava, as if truly trying to size her up. She gave Frank only the briefest of consideration. "This *would* be the first time I've seen any sort of energy or effort from the police to solve a crime against an immigrant," she admitted. "Did you know Eve or something?"

"No ma'am," Ava answered. "A woman has been killed, and the killer got away. As a member of the NYPD, it's our responsibility to find the killer before he strikes again. Immigrant or not, a murder has been committed and I intend to find the murderer.

This was apparently enough to convince Maggie. She sighed heavily and asked: "So what do you need from me?"

"Anything you can tell us about her," Frank said. "We know her father has left town, and finding him is going to be tricky enough considering he was presumably an illegal. Do you know if she was maybe seeing a man? Sort of like courting anyone?"

"Not that I know of."

"How about the place where she lived?" Ava asked. "Did you ever visit her?"

"From time to time. More often than not, we ran into one another in the alleys—doing laundry, keeping the young ones in line."

"Children?" Ava asked. "Who did the children belong to?"

"Hell if I know. There's a lot of 'em that run around here. We just try to keep them out of trouble."

"Did the kids like her?" Frank asked.

"Most of the time. She was sweet, but strict, too."

Ava looked directly into the old woman's eyes and could tell that, despite her willingness to help, she was still nervous to be speaking with them. "Ma'am, I need you to be as honest as possible, even if it means another immigrant could get into trouble. Can you think of *anyone* that would have any reason to kill Eve?"

"No. I've given that some thought myself and I come up with nothing. Everyone she was sharing that building with pretty much adored her. She'd gotten a job, was doing what she could to make sure she lived a respectable life. Trying to get an actual start in this city, you know?"

"What about people that helped her get stable?" Frank asked. "Do you know how she got into the city in the first place? Maybe someone that helped her find space in her tenement?"

For just a split second, Ava thought she saw something like fear in Maggie's eyes. This was a question she had not been expecting but might very well have the answer to all the same. But the fear was gone right away as the old lady pushed it down.

"No, I'm sorry."

"Please," Ava said "If you could—"

"Now, I've told you all I know," she said, almost regrettably. "I believe it's time for you to leave."

Ava could tell that Frank wasn't quite ready to take this suggestion. He was starting to look frustrated. Maybe he'd also seen that glimmer of fear and acknowledgement in her eyes and knew she was holding out on them. But Ava also knew that this woman had fought every possible instinct to invite them into her home and tell them anything at all. Besides that, Ava had another idea, spurred on by Frank's previous question.

"Of course," Ava said. "Thank you so much for your time."

She started for the door and when it was clear Frank had no intention of doing so, Ava reached out and took him by the wrist. He resisted at first but relented when he met her eyes. When they were back out on the street, Ava could tell that Frank was doing his very best not to seem frustrated. It was present in the way he spoke to her, the words chipped and carefully considered.

"You know she really told us next to nothing."

"That's not true. She told us she found it unlikely that anyone in the immigrant community around here would have killed Eve."

He opened his mouth to argue the point but then closed it and smiled thinly. "You wouldn't just give up so easily unless you knew something—unless you got something from that whole lot of nothing in there. What is it?"

"What you asked her…about how Eve got here."

"What about it?"

"Well, for all immigrants—legal and illegal alike—I'd assume there aren't but so many connection points to get into the city. And Eve isn't the only one we know that was attacked, remember?"

"Wanda Polanski."

"That's right. So I think we pay her a visit and ask her the same question. Even if everything is on the level with her, I bet we'd be able to find some nooks and crannies in the process where less-than-reputable people are looking to make a quick buck on the despair of so many immigrants."

Frank considered it, nodding slowly. "It's certainly worth a shot."

As they headed back to the car, Ava felt just as lost on the case as before but now they at least had a new door to look behind. There were answers out there somewhere and a killer that was linked to them.

CHAPTER TWENTY

Mr. Milner was just as helpful as he had been the day before, allowing them to speak with Wanda without any hassle or obstacles. Wanda, though, didn't seem as eager to help as the day before. When she approached them in the front of the garment factory and sat down with them, she seemed almost resentful.

"Is this going to be a regular thing now?" Wanda asked. "If you can't find answers, you keep harassing other immigrants that had nothing to do with your case?"

"I certainly hope not," Ava said, trying her best to not take the comment personally. "We do need to ask you just a few more quick questions, though. And hopefully it will help us find the killer of an innocent woman."

"I already answered all of your questions yesterday."

"Yes, but now we have new ones," Frank said. "This case is starting to feel a bit bigger than we originally assumed."

Ava followed up before giving Wanda time to argue. "One of the remaining questions we have about the victim is how she came to be in the city in the first place. We're wondering if she had connections that helped her get into the city, find housing, a job, and all of that. But since you were also attacked by someone while at Ellis Isle, we started to wonder the same about you—and if there might be a connection there."

Wanda looked at them both as if they were idiots. Clearly, she was not about to reveal her status: legal, illegal, in the process of becoming legal. It was enough to make Ava think she was illegal and, quite honestly, she did not care.

Apparently, Frank sensed the same thing. He opened his hands in a strange gesture, as if to show his hands were empty, that he was here to help. "I'll level with you. We don't give a damn if you're here illegally. I mean that honestly. It's not important to our case and it's not why we're here. We just need answers and right now, you may be the only person that can give them."

The same sort of fear that had crept into Mrs. Maggie's eyes flashed briefly into Wanda's. Ava hated that there was so much fear and distrust among this community—even those that had managed to make a proper new beginning for themselves.

"No one around here—none of the immigrants I know as friends or coworkers—trust the cops. I'm already getting sideways glances form the gals in the back from talking to you the first time."

"I understand that," Frank said. "And we hope closing this case will prove to the community that we truly are here to help."

"We just want to find this killer," Ava pleaded. "We won't mention your name at all if it's needed during the course of the investigation."

"Why should I trust you?"

Ava countered with a question of her own. "Why would we come to you a second time for answers? Do you think we enjoy it, retreading the same places we've already looked in an area where we know we aren't trusted? I want to close this case and I need your help with it. If you and so many others want to see a shift in the relationship between immigrants and police, it can start here, with you."

Wanda hung her head for a moment. When she looked back to them, Ava thought she saw the beginnings of tears in the woman's eyes.

"His name is Aaron Scully. He's an immigrant, too, though I'm not quite sure from where."

"And what did he do to help you?"

"He said he had inside people at Ellis Island and in the city government. He said he could make sure I was able to skip the fees with all the paperwork and that he'd make sure I had a place to stay right away."

"Did he come through on those promises?" Ava asked.

"At first." Wanda struggled to continue on and now Ava could clearly see the glistening of tears in the corners of her eyes. "Once I got settled in to the dump he found for me, he started asking for payment. And because he knew I didn't have money, he asked for other things. Sexual things."

"How long was this after you met him?" Ava asked, already feeling a flurry of anger rising up inside of her.

"Maybe two weeks. And before you start judging me, I only agreed once. When he came back a second time, I refused. He said he'd see to it that I was removed from the building I was in and that he'd stop looking for work for me. He left me and I only saw him one other time. He came by my building, and I thought he was going to force me to…to you know. But there were some other women there, and they helped fend him off."

"And you never reported this?"

Wanda chuckled in a sarcastic way and said: "To who?"

"Do you think he might have been the man that attacked you when you were out on Ellis Isle?" Frank asked.

"I don't know, but I've wondered about that myself. I mean…he knew where to find me. It was like he'd been looking specifically for me."

"Where *did* he first approach you?" Ava asked.

"Two days after I was attacked. I was sleeping in an alley, begging for food. I asked him for some money or food or *anything* and he said he could help me. And he did—I'll give him that. For a while, anyway."

Ava thought it over, thinking that a man that operated from such a position—whether it was legitimate or fabricated—could really hold a great deal of power over desperate immigrants. Especially females that had come to America without any family.

"You said he was also an immigrant," Frank said. "Did he tell you that?"

"Yes. He was telling the truth. He showed me his papers."

"Have you spoken to anyone else that he supposedly helped?" Ava asked.

"A few. One woman seemed very surprised that I had accused him if acting the way that he did. But there were two others that knew exactly what I was talking about. One of them, I believe, still sees him from time to time."

Ava had never even laid eyes on the man, and she hated him already. Even if he was not their killer, he needed to be stopped. But based on Wanda's story, Ava supposed he could very well be the killer. He seemed to know where to find women and had no respect for them. It was as good a place to start as any, she supposed.

"Do you know where we can find this man?"

"You'll probably find him down by the docks, on the East River." She seemed hesitant to tell them. Her voice was soft and trembling. She looked away as she said it, as if ashamed or embarrassed. "He told me that's where he can find both sorts of people: Americans in need of workers, and immigrants looking for any means possible to find work and get into the country properly."

"Thank you. And don't worry…we won't tell him we heard about him from you."

Wiping a tear from her eye, Wanda said, "I don't care. In fact, if you end up arresting him, I think I'd *like* for you tell him."

Ava couldn't stop the thin smile that touched her lips. "Well then I'll make sure to do that if we get the chance."

CHAPTER TWENTY ONE

Frank was quickly learning that Ava was an exceptional detective. This was made all the more impressive by the fact that she'd never had any formal training. From Day One, she'd simply been tossed into the deep end and told that she damn well better learn to swim or she was going to drown. He'd learned to start trusting her instincts and listening to her ideas and theories with a lot more focus than when they'd first met.

Yet as they made their way back out to the car, he could not wrap his head around why Ava had been so eager to leave Wanda behind. There wasn't nearly enough reason to cut the questioning short and go after a guy that was clearly only looking for clever ways to get sexual favors from women. Was it deplorable? Hell yes. But they were looking for a killer. He sometimes wondered if Ava took the whole sexual equality thing far too seriously and let it warp her view of certain aspects of cases.

"So, I'm going to ask you this," he said as they got into the car. "And I need you to know this is not me trying to tell you that you're wrong."

"A great way to start a conversation," she joked.

"I can't help but wonder if you're so eager to go after this Aaron Scully guy just because he's preying on women. Sure, he needs to be found and stopped, but we can send someone else to do that; he's not really part of our investigation."

"We don't know that."

He turned east, doing his best to remain respectful as he continued to question her. "For the sake of conversation, why do you think it's worth looking at Scully as a suspect?"

"Because he's not only trying to victimize these women. He's approaching this all with the belief that once he's helped them, they owe him something. And being helpless women new to this foreign place, they'd do pretty much anything. A man that thinks he's owed something from a woman that then doesn't get it…well, I've seen for myself, as a woman, how that sometimes goes."

"Yeah, but even if Aaron Scully is the guy that tried killing Wanda at Ellis Island, why the hell would he then approach her and ask her if she needed help?"

"You don't think it's him, then?"

"I'm not saying that. There's a lot about him that fits, for sure. I just don't think we can pin the hope of the entire case on him. I feel like there might be something missing…something we haven't thought of yet."

Ava thought this over and seemed displeased with it. She then went on, as if she had totally dismissed Frank's slight objection. "Maybe he couldn't get what he wanted the first time," Ava said. "He wasn't able to kill her, so he wanted to have his way with her some other way. Forgive me for demeaning your sex to such simplistic terms, but for men like that it comes down to control."

He understood where she was coming from. A lot of the pieces did indeed line up and point to Scully, but Frank still thought her own personal journey might be clouding her judgement. But maybe she was right. It was certainly worth pursuing, at the very least. Besides, even if Aaron Scully turned out to be a waste of their time, maybe the location itself would produce some fruit.

They remained quiet a bit longer as the discussion lingered between them. Frank glanced over to her from time to time, watching as she looked out of the window. He liked to watch her think; it was almost as if he could actually hear gears grinding in her head. He was attracted to her in the first place, but when she went deep into thought there was a whole new beauty to her that ensnared him all over again.

When they arrived at the docks, Frank couldn't help but feel a little out of his element. He knew most of the city well enough, but this was one area he wasn't overly familiar with. Immediately after they parked, they walked by a few small stands where people were selling fresh fish. Much further along, with the smell of fish and stagnant water filling the air, they came to where a few cargo ships had parked along the edge of the docks. Crews were working to unload the ships, streams of people going in and then coming out with crates to divvy out on the docks and waiting platforms.

"If Scully came out here to recruit, I doubt he's doing it in any official capacity," Frank said. "Asking people working on the boats isn't going to net anything." He grinned, waiting to see if she got the little pun.

He was rewarded with only a quick grin. "You think maybe the stalls back near the road, with the fish-peddlers?" she asked.

"Yeah, that's more likely."

They headed back that way, both of them scanning the thickening groups of people along the sidewalks and peering out near the river. Frank was looking for a man that might be holding an audience with one or two others, maybe off to the side in a hushed conversation. He saw nothing of the sort, though. There was just too much going on, too many people eager for food and work.

They approached the first of several fish-selling setups. The station was flooded with people anxious for fresh catches, but Frank was not at all surprised when Ava subtly muscled her way through the crowd and directly up to the proprietor. He followed behind her, noticing that he got a series of annoyed looks as he passed, whereas people seemed to naturally step out of the way for the pretty young woman.

"Excuse me, sir," he heard Ava ask the seller, showing her badge quickly. "I'm looking for a gentleman by the name of Scully. Aaron Scully. He's believed to spend a lot of time down here. Does that name ring a bell?"

The man was clearly very busy, currently in the process of wrapping up a pair of decent-looking salmon. He did seem to think about the name for a moment and then shook his head. "Can't say that it does. But go to the end of this row and ask Clancy—he'll be the fella down there scaling and gutting."

Ava nodded her thanks and slipped out of the crowd just as easily as she'd joined it. Frank followed her and realized that he was starting to not mind taking the back seat whenever Ava slipped to the in-charge position. It was more than just his attraction to her; it was seeing without a doubt that she was not only growing but evolving in her position as a detective. He truly was starting to see her as *just* a fellow dick rather that a *female* detective.

They came to the end of the row of little stalls and set-ups, the air pungent with a variety of different fish. Just as the first proprietor had said, there was a man sitting in a wooden chair, hunched over a pile of fish. He was short and portly, his brown hair a messy mop on his head. The fish and many of their insides were scattered over sections of old newspaper. The man—presumably Clancy—was working on the fish with expert skill and precision. He was moving so fast as he slid the knife up the gullet of a fresh one that Frank barely even saw the motion. The fish was split open like a hot roll, its insides waiting and exposed.

He glanced up at Frank and Ava as they approached. Ava stepped to the side, allowing Frank to move closer to the man. "Howdy, sir," Frank said. "Would you happen to be Clancy?"

"A'yuh, that's me. If you need some filets, you're just gonna have to wait; I already got a few folks on my waiting list."

"No filets for me, I'm afraid. We were told you were a man that knows just about everyone."

Clancy smiled proudly and nodded. "That I am. Who you looking for?"

Frank showed his badge, and Clancy was still able to remove the guts of the fish while looking at it. "We're looking for a man by the name of Aaron Scully. We understand he hangs out around the docks quite often."

"He sure does. And you know, I've seen him a few times already this morning." For the first time since they'd seen him, Clancy's knife stopped moving as he looked up and to the right. He remained in his seat, craning his neck over the crowd. And then, with a knife smeared with scales and gore, he pointed in that direction. "Why, that's him right there."

Frank followed the direction of the blade and saw a man of average build. He was dressed in a respectable-looking coat similar to what some of the detectives down at the station wore. As it just so happened, Aaron Scully was looking in their direction at the same time Clancy pointed him out. And he did not look thrilled to be called out in such a way. He looked mad at first, and then slightly alarmed.

Slowly, Frank put his badge away and thanked Clancy without taking his eyes from Scully. He took one step away from the fish-butcher, and then another. And that's when Aaron Scully apparently decided he didn't want to stick around. He was roughly ten yards away, standing on the other side of the crowded dock when Frank started walking slowly over to him. Scully then also took a hurried step in the other direction, and then another.

"Yeah, he's not liking that we're here," Ava said from behind.

Frank took another step and this time, Scully responded by breaking into a sprint. Frank muttered a curse under his breath and took off after him. He nearly collided with a man standing in front of him and turned to make sure Ava was able to make it out of the throng of people in front of the fish sellers. When he saw that she was in the clear and rushing up behind him, Frank turned back around, spotted Scully still on the move, and gave chase. Up ahead, Scully moved along through the crowd like a man that was very familiar with the area.

Frank did his best to keep up but was afraid that one wrong step would end the chase and the first plausible lead they had would get away.

CHAPTER TWENTY TWO

It wasn't the mingling crowds of people that annoyed Ava the most as they chased after Aaron Scully—it was the often-thin amount of space in which they had to chase him. As they followed Scully off of the docks and toward a small side street that ran along the river, Ava was very aware that two stray steps to the left and she could end up in the water. And if not her, then some unfortunate individual that might happen to get in the way of their chase.

Fortunately, Frank was in the lead and most people stepped aside quickly for him. She did hear a few people mutter their complaints as they passed, and she even heard something splash down into the river off the side of the dock. She turned to see if this was a person but saw nothing but a curious crowd watching on behind her.

As they came near the end of the dock, another wooden walkway balanced along the edge of the river and solid ground. It diverted out into a T-intersection and Ava was just barely able to see Scully ahead of them, taking a hard right. Frank did the same and when he did, he nearly fell down, slipping on the slick surface of the dock. She was sure he was going to crash and burn but he managed to right himself and continue on.

They ran onto the secondary dock that led out into the street. There was a short set of stairs that led up to a side street—the sort of street where delivery trucks would pick up and drop off deliveries. There weren't a lot of people on the sidewalks or in the road itself, but there *were* a lot of automobiles. Seeing this, she realized that there were now any number of ways for Scully to hide from them. If he could get another few feet ahead of them, he could simply disappear.

But as they came to the stairs, Ava looked to her left and saw the coat Scully was wearing. He was dodging around a truck with a wooden bed on the back, currently being filled by two men with a pushcart.

"Frank! Over there!"

Her shout caused him to correct his direction, as he was angling to the right as they came to the top of the stairs.

"You sure?" Frank asked.

"Positive."

He changed direction, the slight stall allowing Ava to draw up closer beside him. They were now running toe to heel, practically glued to one another as they made their way down the sidewalk. They were still having to dodge the occasional pedestrian and Frank had to shove one stubborn man out of the way.

They ran along the street, the rover to their left, the buildings, warehouses and side streets to their right. Scully still had a considerable lead on them—about twelve or fifteen yards if Ava had to guess. If Scully knew the area better than they did, there was a very good chance he was going to get away from them. She was already running at a full sprint and if Frank didn't have another gear hidden deep down within him, this might not end the way she wanted.

A brief flicker of hope came when Scully bolted hard to the right, crossing the street. Someone in a car laid down on their horn. The screeching of brakes and a very loud curse from the driver followed. Scully missed being hit by the automobile by less than six inches; it was frightful enough to him to cause a momentary bit of shock.

And that was the only window of opportunity they needed.

With the car already stopped, Frank blasted across the street without any hesitation, Ava following closely behind. They closed the distance quickly and Ava watched as Frank reached out to grab Scully from behind. Yet, at the very same moment, a man came out of one of the warehouse doors, carrying a crate against his chest. He did not see Frank, and Frank just barely saw him in time. The two men collided, Frank slamming into him and sending them both to the ground, The wooden crate fell to the street, cracking and tumbling.

"What the bleeding hell are you doing?" the man screamed.

Ava thought she heard a muttered apiology as Frank started getting back to his feet. But Ava barely saw or heard this; she was still sprinting forward, heading hard to the right and back in the direction of the river. He made it back across the street but, in shifting directions, made the mistake of letting up just the slightest bit, thinking the chase was over now that Frank had been temporarily sidelined. When he saw Ava still coming for him, he dug in yet again and started running forward. But because Ava had not stopped like he had, the renewed chase was over before it even had a proper chance to begin.

Ava reached out and grabbed him by the shoulder. She was running too fast to come to a proper stop, so she had to shove him hard to the side or fall on top of him. She did her best to simply slam him down onto the sidewalk. He might bust up his chin, but it was much better than both of them tripping and stumbling from the street, down the shallow bank and into the river.

But Ava did not know her own strength. When she pushed him down, she did so with the force of a boxer throwing a right-handed jab. Scully went sprawling forward. He struck a small wooden rail that led to the stairs that worked their way back down to the docks, but when he rebounded from it, he went the wrong way. His eyes grew large, and he let out a shriek of surprise as the open air greeted him. And then, just a moment later, he was in the water. The splash was loud enough to attract the attention of everyone in the area.

"Damn," Ava said, grimacing down to the sight of Scully coming back up to the surface of the murky water. People all around were pointing and laughing. She was so distracted by all of this that she was barely aware of Frank coming up beside her.

"Well," he said with a nervous chuckle. "That's one way to do it, I guess."

"Sorry. I sort of got out of hand."

"No need to apologize," Frank said, doing everything he could to hold back a grin. "But let's fish him out of the water before we make more of a scene."

Ava followed him down the stairs as Aaron Scully bobbed in the water, gasping for breath.

***

It took the help of a fisherman with a net, but they were able to get Aaron Scully out of the river without much of a problem. When Scully was back on the dock, he did his absolute best to play the victim, wanting to make sure the gathered crowd knew what had happened to him.

"What's the meaning of this?" He was soaked and red in the face, somewhere between terrified and angry.

"Let's start by you deciding to run when two detectives came walking your way," Frank said.

"What? Hey, I had no idea you were cops."

"Then why did you run?"

"Because Clancy was pointing and…and you were…I mean…" It was clear that he wasn't going to be able to offer a whole or relevant response.

"Here's the deal," Ava said, leaning in so as few people as possible would hear. "We have some questions to ask you. Make it harder than

107

it has to be, and we'll cuff you in front of each and every one of these people. But if you play nice, you can just walk down to the other end of the docks with us, where there aren't so many ears, and we'll take it from there."

Scully seemed surprised that he was being given an option. Maybe that's why he got to his feet, looking back and forth between the detectives with a degree of skepticism. Frank nodded to the other end of the dock they had fished him out of, to where there were fewer people, just a few boats docked by the edge.

"What is it you want to know?" Scully asked. He dripped along the dock as he walked between Frank and Ava.

Ava said nothing until they'd made it a decent distance away from the larger portion of the crowd that had gathered for the spectacle before she said anything.

"We've gotten information that you take it upon yourself to lend your help to immigrants when they get to the city—especially if they seem to be having trouble with becoming legal, getting a place to stay, or a job. Would that be correct?"

"Sometimes, yes. Is there something wrong with helping people?"

"Absolutely not," Ava said. "But I think the payment you're asking for is a little much."

His cheeks grew even more red, and his lips drew tight. It was enough physical confirmation that the accusations they'd heard from Wanda were at least partially correct.

"But that's not why we're here," Frank said. Ava didn't like that Frank revealed this so soon, but kept quiet. "We're here," Frank went on, "because we believe one of the women you offered to help recently was murdered two days ago."

"Oh my God," he said. "Do you know her name?"

"Eve Buzek."

Even Ava couldn't deny the look of shock on Scully's face. He stared at both of them as if he were waiting for them to reveal that they were just kidding. When it was clear they weren't, he shook his head. "Someone killed her?"

"Yes," Ava said. "Are you saying you did know her?"

"Not well. I just helped with her papers and lined up a job for her."

"And what about payment?" Ava asked. "Don't deny it."

"I asked and she said no, okay?" he snapped. "After that, I left her alone."

Ava wanted to ask why he didn't just leave Wanda alone when she turned him down but didn't want to reveal the woman's name. She had, after all, promised Wanda that her name would not be mentioned.

"How many times did you meet with her?" Frank asked.

Panicked and realizing just what was at stake, Scully started to look very worried. When he spoke, he made sure to get his words right, each one coming slowly and with purpose. "Including the time I first approached her, three times."

"And when was the last time you saw her?" Ava asked.

"I don't know for sure. Maybe two weeks?"

Ava wasn't sure she bought it, though she did think his expressions and reactions were genuine. She knew very well that she did not yet have the instincts necessary to truly read a suspect's face, but she thought she could read Scully's fairly well.

"Where were you two days ago?" Frank asked.

"What time of the day?"

"All day. Can you account for your whereabouts between six in the morning and two in the afternoon?"

"Yeah, yeah, easily. Hell, you can go back and ask Clancy. He saw me. I was here first thing in the morning, like I am most mornings."

"And what about later in the day?" Ava asked.

"I had left the docks and gone about a block and a half west. It's too risky offering help here on the docks. People get sore about helping immigrants sometimes, you know? So I was up there, helping some folks that just got off the boat—ones that sort of skipped Ellis, you know?"

"Can anyone back that up?"

"Yeah, sure, I just don't know how forthcoming they'll be. I worked with at least five or six folks that evening. Talk to a guy named Terry that works over at Wayland Brother's Textiles if you need proof. I got three folks jobs with him. Him and all those people, and then Clancy. Yeah, there's plenty that will back it up."

Ava looked to Frank and saw that he could also feel yet another potential lead slipping away. If he was truly a block and a half away from where they currently stood when Eve was killed, that put him nearly a mile and a half away from the crime scene. There was that, plus the fact that a man that was not quite agile enough to keep from falling into the river did not exactly come off as a capable killer.

"What do you get out of this, exactly?" Frank asked. "Helping immigrants find jobs and shelter, and helping them skirt the law?'

"Other than the occasional sexual favor, of course," Ava said, unable to help herself.

She hated that he actually cringed a bit at the comment, as if she had offended him. "I get a cut from the people that hire them. I mean, they're saving a lot of money by hiring immigrants. Same for the people that build those tenements."

"You're a real hood, you know that?" Ava said.

"Lady, there are people in this town that make money in *far* worse ways."

"Oh, I'm aware of that." She leaned in closer and sensed that Frank was ready to reach out and stop her if she acted out violently. "But let me tell you this. We're going to check up on your alibis. And even if you come out clean as a rose, I swear that if I ever hear about you trying to use the promise of jobs or safety to get a woman's favor, I'll personally hunt you down and take your balls. Do you hear me?"

"You can't talk to me like th—"

She leaned even closer, and she could feel the fire burning in her eyes—so she knew he damn well saw it. "I asked: *Do you hear me?*"

"Yes!"

Trembling in anger, Ava stood upright. Frank took her gently by the arm and led her away. "C'mon, Gold."

She did, and willingly. With the little chase scene and then the suspect splashing in the river, they'd caused enough of a scene today. And not only that, it all seemed to be for no real reason at all. Because yet again, they had come to what appeared to be a dead end and no clear direction to go next.

CHAPTER TWENTY THREE

It had not been easy to find a job, even with some of the more seasoned immigrants taking her in and trying to help her. When she'd finally landed one, Edith Lange had been appreciative and had accepted the meager pay and deplorable hours. She'd heard all about how America—New York City, in particular—was the Land of Opportunity, and she was not about to let an opportunity to work and start a new life slip away, long hours and grueling work be damned.

Her shift at the cotton mill started at three in the afternoon and ended at midnight. If she wanted, she could also have the three-to-nine shift. And though she knew it would only wear her down, she was thinking of taking it as she headed out of the crowded apartment building she'd been living in for the last two weeks. She'd had one those back-to-back shifts three times last week and had ended up sleeping most of Sunday just to recuperate.

Edith Lange was no fool; she knew those shifts were only being offered to her because she worked for much less pay than local citizens. But she also knew that if she complained about this, she'd easily lose her job and would be replaced by any number of immigrants that were desperately seeking work.

So she hurried out of her home and into the alleyway that hid her front door from the street. There were several tenements like this along her little row, as if the entrances into their dwellings were so appalling that they needed to be hidden from the street. She had no delusions about the state of her current home; it was an absolute dump and yes, she was a little embarrassed by it. But she knew this was the hand she'd been dealt. She'd known she would have an uphill battle to start from the moment she'd left her home in Dusseldorf.

She sighed, feeling the aching throbs on her aching hands, prepared for the taxing work ahead. Feeling those aches and pains, she thought it might be a bit of wishful thinking to even consider taking that second shift. She had to think of taking care of herself as well as making money. If she worked herself to death, what was the point in coming from Germany to America?

Edith made it roughly halfway down the alley before she realized she'd left her work gloves back at home. They were already wearing thin (and had been hand-me-downs from another worker to start with) but without them, she was going to rub her fingers raw—and getting blood in the cotton would surely be justification for being fired.

She doubled back quickly, entering the alleyway again and rushing into the apartment. No one was there right now, aside from the old, sick man from Italy. He was in a back corner, separated from the rest of them by a rickety plywood wall that Edith and two others that occupied the space had built on their first day there. Even as Edith hurried through the front door and to the small table in the back corner of the main room, she could hear his raspy breaths behind the wall.

Edith grabbed the gloves and stuffed them deep into the pockets of her well-worn coat. She dashed outside in such a hurry, not wanting to be late for her shift, that she nearly collided with a man that was passing by in front of the building. Apparently, he was using it as a shortcut to save some time.

"My goodness, I'm so sorry," Edith said.

The man seemed irritated at first but, seeing her state and the fact that she was clearly stressed out, offered her a wan smile. "That's okay. You be careful, yeah?"

Edith nodded, embarrassed, and hurried on her way once again. Or, rather, she tried to. She made it one single step before she was stopped. There was an immense pressure at her neck—something soft but, at the same time, oddly insistent. She tried to turn to see what had captured her from behind, but she was unable to do so. Something hard pressed against her knees and she went to the ground, right there on the doorstep to the place she was currently calling home.

As she sank to the ground, the pressure around her neck grew tighter, stronger. She slapped at it with her hands and felt something soft. Some sort of fabric. She tried to get her hands under it, but it was impossible. And as her vision grew hazy and her face felt both hot and cold all at the same time, her lungs started to scream for air.

But there was none to be had. There was only the presence of the man behind her, and she could vaguely recall a comment spoken less than thirty seconds ago.

"That's okay. You be careful, yeah?"

It was him. That same man. And for some reason, he was taking her life. Thinking this, the idea came crashing through her with sudden clarity and she spent her last ten seconds of life fighting valiantly. She reached back, slapping at the man, even lacing one good blow. But ultimately, he never let go.

Edith Lange ran out of breath and died on the doorstep of a rundown place that was supposed to signify the first step and promising journey. But that journey ended far too soon. The last thing she saw was the dirty floor of the alleyway and the shadow of the man standing behind her—the man that had taken her breath, her life, and the promise of a new beginning.

CHAPTER TWENTY FOUR

Ava figured it would be a complete and utter waste of time to go back to the precinct. What would they do there? Dive back into records and ultimately find nothing? No, she knew their best bet was to head back to the area where Eve had been killed—where so many hopeful immigrants were trying to get another go at life. And with Aaron Scully's alibis turning out to be absolutely true (strongly backed up by their fish-gutting friend, Clancy) they had no time to waste.

Somehow, they were starting from the bottom again.

"Can you imagine it?" Ava asked, looking out of the passenger side window as Frank drove back into the Lower East Side.

"Imagine what?" he said.

"Hearing about this wondrous new city overseas—this place where you can go and start your life over. A place full of dreams and possibilities. And then this is what you get." She gestured out of the window, the packed streets and the filthy buildings, streets that were little more than dirty passageways. "I know it may sound naïve, but we need to do better."

"We?" Frank said.

"The police."

He nodded but seemed to have nothing else to say in the moment.

"I wonder if we're a little off base with our thinking," she added. "I hate to think such a thing but what if the killer is a fellow immigrant? Maybe someone down on his luck and can't get a job—so he's trying to thin the herd a bit, making sure he has a better chance."

"Could be," Frank said. "Both women did have jobs. But if it's an immigrant that's going after these women, I think that decreases our chances of finding him."

"We could maybe start with—"

But she stopped here, the comment caught in her throat. Off to the right, on Frank's side of the car, she saw a man standing at the corner of an alleyway and the street. He was shouting something that she could not hear over the car's engine. A few people had stopped to see what he was saying, but most walked on. There were two people standing near him, though. One looked down the alleyway and when they turned back to the shouting man, their eyes were wide, their mouth agape.

"Frank, stop."

"What?"

"Something's going on over there." She nodded in the direction of the shouting man and the slack-jawed passerby.

Frank did indeed bring the car to a stop but there wasn't immediate parking available. He grunted as he scanned the sides of the street for a place to park.

"Meet me there as soon as you can. Might be nothing. But…"

She gave a shrug and got out of the car. She crossed the street and angled herself over toward the shouting man. She peered behind her and watched as Frank inched along in search of a parking space.

Ava approached the man and saw that he looked incredibly tired, almost to the point of appearing ill. He looked at Ava for just a moment before his eyes widened. The person standing beside him gave her a peculiar glance, clearly thinking she had no business on this side of town.

"What is it, sir?" Ava asked. "What are you screaming about?"

She showed her badge, not knowing if it would do any good or not. The man that had been screaming barely even looked at it as he pointed back down the alleyway.

"She's dead! Someone killed her right on the doorstep!"

Ava didn't bother asking questions. She wedged herself between the screaming man and the bystander. As she did so, she noticed a heavy wheeze to the screaming man's breath. Maybe he *was* sick.

Ava saw the body right away, just the legs at first because the body was laying down on the doorstep of a decrepit tenement dwelling. She saw more as she got closer—a hand, the arm, the chest. Finally approaching the entrance to the dwelling, she then saw the entire body. It was a woman that looked to be somewhere near thirty. Her bright, blue eyes were open, staring to the side, as if studying the brick wall of the neighboring building.

She was not pale, and when Ava reached out to touch the woman's cheek, she found it still warm. This woman had died very recently. The sick, shouting man came rushing back to her, leaning against the wall for support.

"Do you know this woman?" Ava asked.

"Yes! Been living with her for about two weeks now, I have." Hearing more of the man's clipped speech, she thought him to be German.

"What's her name?"

"Edith."

"And when did you find her body?" Ava asked.

"No more'n five minutes ago."

"Do you know why she might have been in the alley?"

"Probably heading to work. I think she had a three o' clock shift down at the cotton mill today."

Ava looked up and down the alleyway. To think that the killer had been there within the last five or ten minutes was maddening. As she looked back down toward the street, she saw Frank hurrying along. When he spotted the body beside Ava, he broke into a run.

"This man discovered the body five minutes ago," Ava said. "She's still warm, Frank. This was recent."

Frank pointed to the woman's neck, indicating the slight discoloration. It almost looked as if someone had slapped her all around the neck. There was no bruising, but the flesh was a very angry red.

"Strangled," Ava said. Then, looking to the sick man, she asked: "Did you see anyone else in the alley when you found her?"

"No. No one." He was leaning against the side of the building, exhausted from the last few minutes.

"Sir, get back inside. You clearly don't need to be out here."

He nodded, wiping a tear away. "You'll find who did this?"

"We're going to try our absolute best."

The sick man nodded only vaguely, as if he really didn't believe her. When he slunk back into the building, he closed the door behind him. The weak doorframe shook with the effort.

"No more than ten minutes has passed," Ava said, getting to get feet. "He's nearby."

Frank looked up and down the alleyway, clearly deep in thought. "Okay, so you make the call, Gold."

She wasn't sure how she felt about him calling her *Gold*, even while on the job. Things felt different between them now and the use of her last name felt so impersonal. "What call?"

"Run quick laps around these next few blocks to find anyone that looks out of place or suspicious, or find the nearest telephone to call this in to the station."

It was an easy answer, one that made her feel angry all over again. "I'll look for suspects. If I call this in and it's treated as a non-issue, I'm going to blow my top."

"Okay. I'll let the sick man know that we have to leave her here for now. Let's meet back here in half an hour. You good with that?"

Ava nodded, her mind already on the hunt ahead of her. No witnesses, no leads…it wouldn't be much of a hunt. Hell, even if the killer was standing on the street just off of the alley, they'd have no way of knowing it was him. For the sake of feeling productive, though, she had to at least try.

"Hey, Gold?" Frank said.

She turned back to him, biting back a comment about his choice of name for her in the past two minutes. "Yeah?"

"Keep your cool. Try not to knock anyone else down. Particularly into a river."

She didn't even bother with a fake smile. "I make no promises."

She turned her back and started down the alley, her feet crunching the filth and grit underfoot as she marched out in search of a killer.

CHAPTER TWENTY FIVE

The half an hour of searching netted zero results. When she returned to the murder scene, she wasn't surprised to see only Frank there. Apparently, another dead immigrant was not going to be a cause of rushing or emergency for the police. She did see that Frank had covered the body with an old blanket, giving Edith at least some sort of respect in her death.

"Nothing?" he asked her as she joined him on the doorstep.

"No. No one. I may be getting some instincts, but I can't tell a killer by just looking at him."

"None of us can."

"What was the precinct response?"

"Someone will be here shortly apparently. But that was—" he stopped and checked his watch. "Sixteen minutes ago, and so far, I've seen no one. I did knock on the door and speak to our sick friend, though. Learned a bit more about the victim."

"Like what?"

"Like her name is Edith Lange. She came here a little over two weeks ago, from Dusseldorf. She did have some helping find a job, but he doesn't know who helped her. She's also completely legal. Her papers were inside, with some family keepsakes. The sick man was very quick to show me all of it."

"So she's here legally?"

"Yes. Since day one, she's been legal."

"I wonder if the killer knew."

"I was thinking the same thing. If we have a killer that is targeting *any* kind of immigrant and not just illegals, this case just got a lot harder. And I don't see Minard allowing another day on this if that's the case."

"But there are two bodies now. Two women, killed by the same person."

Frank nodded and opened his hand to the empty alley around them. "And look how much the police care."

An overwhelming feeling of defeat came rushing over her. She'd felt helplessness before, and she was all too familiar with feeling like a case had gotten away from her. But she was feeling this one on a deeper level, perhaps because she knew that if she and Frank couldn't figure this case out, no one else was going to care enough to pick it up and run with it. And with two women now dead and another having been attacked previously, she was fairly certain this trend would continue. The killer would kill another and another, and if the killer was never found, she'd forever feel responsible for those deaths.

And don't forget, some teasing voice in her head said. *You can't find Clarence's killer, either. And let's face it: if you can't find this guy, how do you really expect to ever find the man that killed your husband. With him, you even have a description, and you still can't get it done.*

"Hey…Ava?"

She looked to Frank, realizing that he referred to her a little more personally this time. "I'm fine. I just…I don't even know where to go from here."

"I know it doesn't seem like it, but we're doing everything we can."

Ava knew this, but it was hard to believe it when their second dead victim was at her feet. Ava looked around the alley, looking for similarities in the scenes. There were clotheslines here, too, but they were much farther down the alley. The other similarity, though, was a little more obvious and as she considered it, she couldn't quite figure out why it might be a factor in the murders.

Just like the scene where Eve Buzek was killed, the dead nature of the alley and the fact that the doorstep was out of sight form the street were the same. It indicated that this killer knew the women—that he had studied them, their movements and their schedules. The sick man had said he believed Edith had been on her way to work. It seemed the killer must have known this, too. Maybe that's why he'd been able to strike so blatantly in broad daylight. Maybe he'd known that Eve Buzek would go out to dry her laundry in the alley when she did.

These were all just guesses, but there seemed to be some weight to it. And as she thought it over, Ava couldn't help but once again look up and down the alley. The killer had watched them, maybe even followed them. To think she could have very well passed by him while she'd been looking on the streets while Frank had made a call to the precinct sickened her.

"You asked a question out loud a little while ago," Frank said. "Sort of just wondering out loud. You asked if the killer knew if she was legal or not. And you know…maybe he didn't. And I can't help but wonder if the fact that she didn't have her papers on her made him *assume* she was."

"So most legal immigrants carry their papers on them?"

"From what I've heard, it's pretty common. Someone like this woman, though—with a job and a place to stay and at least some sense of normalcy—maybe she got comfortable and just forgot."

"But it also seems that the killer is staking these women out," Ava pointed out. "He knows their schedules, their routines. It seems like that, anyway…"

"And you think if he knew them that well he would have known Edith was legal?"

"Maybe. And maybe legal or illegal doesn't matter to this guy at all."

But somewhere at the core of that thought, she felt a kernel of promise. Maybe there was something there. She thought of Harvey Jackson, hunting immigrants down and demanding to see their papers as if he was an extension of the law. What if their killer was indeed doing that? What if he *was* only going after illegals and just made an honest mistake when it had come to Edith?

"Ah, look at this," Frank said, looking to the street-end of the alley. "The cavalry."

Ava saw a single uniformed cop walking down the alley. He was younger than she was, so clearly a rookie. He made his way down the alley as if he were disgusted by it. He looked like he feared a monster might jump out around a corner at him at any minute.

"Detectives Wimbly and Gold?" he asked.

"That's us," Frank said.

"I'm here to take down the report for the dead immigrant."

"Minard sent you?" Ava asked.

"He did," the young officer said. "And he seemed irritated about it, too. Now…what exactly do you know about the victim?"

"Name of Edith Lange," Frank said. "Not sure of her age, but she's legal."

"Yeah?" the young officer asked this as if he thought his leg was being pulled.

"Yes. I've seen her papers. They're inside, if you need to see them."

"Any suspects?"

"Not yet," Ava said. "If you have more questions, one of her roommates is just inside."

She started walking away, back to the street. Frank followed her tentatively while the young officer looked on.

"That's it?" the officer said.

"That's it. We found the body, you're the backup. Is forensics on the way?"

"And the coroner."

"Good. Now Detective Wimbly and I need to get out there and find the man that did this. This makes two—and there's a third that was lucky to get away."

"I'll let Minard know," the young officer said as he took a small notebook from his breast pocket. He said it as a threat, but it did not bother Ava in the slightest.

Frank remained quiet until they reached the street. As the evening wore on, the traffic started to thicken a bit. "What are you thinking?" Frank asked her as they crossed the street to where he'd parked the car.

"I'm thinking she was killed close to her home—like right at the front door. And so was Eve. Eve was illegal, yes. And without her papers on her, Edith may as well have been. It makes me wonder if the killer is asking to see papers. And when the women don't have them, he's killing them."

"So who would just go around asking to see their papers—outside of a joker like Harvey Jackson?"

"You're not going to like the answer."

He opened his mouth, perhaps to tell her to let him know anyway. But then she saw the answer register in his eyes. He narrowed his gaze at her and sighed. "You think it's a cop."

"Given the way things have been handled to this point, yes…I'm willing to consider it a strong possibility."

"That's dangerous, Ava."

"So we'll keep it to ourselves."

She could tell that he was uneasy even thinking about the possibility, and she understood it. he'd been molded within the police force; he knew their ways and policies. He was very much a part of the machine. She, however, had come onto the force after much scrutiny and controversy. She had yet to see the brotherhood and positive influence the force was supposed to provide.

"I can't very well go out looking for police and ask about their involvement in the murder of illegal immigrants," Frank said. "So, if you really buy into this theory, you're going to need to figure out a way to do it where it's *very* subtle."

Ava nodded as she looked through the windshield. "I figured as much. And I'm already one step ahead of you."

"Okay. So where are we going?"

"As much as I hate to leave the center of all the action, I think we need to head back to the precinct."

"You're not thinking of kicking the hornet's nest, are you?"

She chuckled, shaking her head. "Why kick it when you can fly right in undetected?"

CHAPTER TWENTY SIX

It was 3:45 when they walked through the precinct doors. Almost right away, they went their separate ways, as was the plan they'd conjured up on the ride over. Ava felt that their plan was actually quite simple and would be seen as pretty standard and effective police work. Frank was headed to Minard's office to fill him on how the case was going so far. He was going to request another day in order to keep up appearances but if he was denied, he would not put up too much of a fight. He'd then head to his desk and start writing up his version of the report in regard to the discovery of Edith Lange's body.

As for Ava, she was heading to Records. If anyone asked why, she would claim that she was looking into any particular block on the Lower East Side that had been responsible for fights or public disturbances. She simply wanted to try to narrow her search down to as small an area as possible—which was a good idea now that she thought of it.

Yet, on the way to Records, Ava stopped. She looked to the door for a moment, wondering if that would really be the best place to get the sort of answers she was looking for. The police had already proved countless times that their attention to detail when it came to crimes against immigrants was lackluster at best. Even if she did find what she was looking for, she figured there would be more questions than answers.

With another idea in mind, Ava turned to her right and headed to the back of the main floor, making her way to the backside of the bullpen. She then took the stairs down to the Women's Bureau. She noted that a few people eyed her as she went but she was used to that by now. She also wondered if anyone that was bothering to watch her might lose interest when they saw where she was headed.

When she arrived down in the Women's Bureau offices, she found only Frances and Lottie. Frances was slightly red in the face, her short hair sweaty and curled. Having trained under Frances, Ava knew this likely meant that she'd just come in from off the streets, maybe on a patrol or to question someone in relation to a crime.

"Ah, look at this," Lottie said as she saw Ava enter the room. "It is our legendary lady hero, come to grace us with her presence."

Ava knew it was all in good fun, so the laughter that came out of her was a bit sarcastic but mostly genuine. "I *have* decided to grace you with my presence," Ava said. "Not only that, I was wondering if either of you might be able to answer some questions about how the force has really been handling things out where most of the immigrants are living."

"Why us?" Frances asked.

"Well, it was because of you that I even heard about Eve Buzek being killed. And by now, I've learned the same thing as you: nothing out there is being taken seriously. Frances, you told me that all of the reports and paperwork for any cases coming out of that area are being sent down here because no one upstairs wants to deal with it, right?"

"Right."

"So I was wondering if you had any other answers I might need in those files you keep in your bottom drawer. I'm looking for the names of any cops that routinely work that beat."

Lottie chuckled at this, reclining in her seat at her desk. "I don't know that you can use the word 'routinely' to describe anything we're currently doing in that part of town."

Ava looked to the office door, making sure it was closed. Even when she saw that it was, she lowered her voice when she started speaking again. "The last two days have showed me not only that we're treating the people out there like garbage, but also that no matter what I do, the bulk of public opinion about me is not going to change upstairs. Frances…I know it's asking a lot, but I'd like to know the names of the officers that are sending down the most paperwork."

Frances cringed a bit, a look that did not go well with her sweaty, red face. "That's actually pretty easy. There are two. Only two. I believe one of them was sent out to meet with you and Frank earlier this evening."

"Oh, the young guy."

"Yeah," Lottie said. "His name is Edwin Griffith. Sort of a bumbling idiot, but I'm anxiously waiting on him to ask me out."

Ignoring Lottie's comment, Frances went on. "But if you're suspecting some sort of foul play, I can tell you right now that Edwin Griffith is not your guy. He's far too concerned with keeping his nose up Minard's backside to even *think* of abusing his power."

"Okay, so who is the other one?" Ava asked.

"A guy named William Duggar. He's the sort that flies under the radar. Been on the force for about ten years, I'd guess."

"He brought in a pair of immigrants a few days ago," Lottie said. "One of them was roughed up pretty bad."

"Duggar roughed them up?"

"Yeah, that was my take of it," Lottie said. "I can also tell you that I've heard him countless times griping about immigrant laws and reforms in the break room. He's pretty vocal about it."

Ava thought it over. William Duggar certainly fit the bill from what she was hearing, but she needed more if she was legitimately going to look into him as being a suspect. To make such a dangerous leap, she'd pretty much need to catch the man with his hands around an immigrant's neck. And even then, it would be an uphill battle.

She was going to have to talk to Frank. When it came to trying to single out a cop as a suspect for such a heinous crime, she wasn't sure how he'd react. But Records would provide nothing for her in that regard and no one else was going to speak bluntly about another officer. So Frank was her only chance.

"Thanks, ladies," she said, heading for the door.

"Gold?...Ava?" Frances said. She sounded concerned, her voice soft and hesitant.

Ava turned and faced the first person in this building to truly give her a chance. "Yes?"

"You have to be careful with this. The way you've shaken things up around here over the past month or so—specially shedding light on a few dirty cops—you don't want to make more enemies."

Ava could only nod. She was thinking that enemies were the last thing she was concerned about when innocent women were being murdered. But that sounded like something a mobster might say and she didn't quite have the weight or confidence to say such a thing to these women anyway.

She went upstairs and made a direct line to Frank's desk. He was rolling a sheet of paper into his typewriter, apparently having just finished up with Minard. He glanced up at her as she parked her butt on the edge of his desk. She made a mental note to maybe set a chair here if he'd allow it.

"How'd it go with Minard?" she asked.

"He's torn. He agrees that a second body makes this a serious issue. But I think he's hesitant to send too many people out that way. I think...I don't know. I think he's expecting something to happen with this whole money thing. People keep acting like the banks are going to fold up and the sky is going to fall."

"I don't give a damn about money right now." she said. "Did he give us more time?"

"Well, he was very careful how he worded things. He didn't officially give us more time, but he also said nothing about taking us off of it. So, having worked with Minard for as long as I have, I know what that means. It means we can still work it, but we need to keep it quiet. And I think the same rules apply as before: if something else comes up, it takes priority." He sighed and then lowered his voice when he asked: "And what about you? Did you find anything?"

"I don't know. I asked the girls downstairs who was sending down the most paperwork—who was sent out to patrol that side of town. She gave me two names and only one seems to really mean much. I was wondering if you might know him."

"Name?"

"William Duggar."

Frank took in a deep breath and let it out as he rested an elbow on his desk, propping his head up in his hands. "Yeah, I know Duggar. The sad thing he's that he's a damn good cop. You might appreciate the fact that he's made several arrests that have weakened the mob. But at the same time…yeah, he's sort of in business for himself. Not the sort of guy you want to just sit down and have a chat with."

"Lottie is pretty sure he roughed up some immigrants being brought in a few weeks back."

"Sounds about right. But Ava…to go after another cop. Are you *trying* to get the entire force pissed at you?"

"No. Besides, no one has to know I'm looking into him. I just need to know if he's on patrol right now. And if he is…where? If it was anywhere near Edith Lange's residence, then I think he's worth a closer look."

"I'll do that for you. I can find out if he's out on patrol. But beyond that…Ava, I just don't know."

She nodded gratefully at him. "I understand. And you…are you going to sit it out?"

"I should. But…well, Duggar can be an ass. Based on things he agrees with and doesn't agree with, I'm going to assume he's not a fan of yours. And I wouldn't put it past him to lash out. So I'm going. But if we get found out, we'll just play it off as a coincidence. We're following up on some leads in the murders of Eve and Edith. Nothing more." He stood up and looked over to the front desk, where visitors checked in and out. It was also where calls came in and where a record of who was patrolling what areas was kept and updated. "You sure about this?"

But she knew even before the question was out of his mouth that he already knew the answer. She could see it in his eyes.

"Yes, I'm sure."

He walked over to the front desk while she slid off of his. She'd learned to appreciate Frank Wimbly as a partner, was starting to appreciate him as a suitor, and now she understood that she was also starting to appreciate him as a man. He had a good heart, though he tried not to let others in the precinct know it. He knew that even in this risky move, going to check on Duggar could cause a lot of friction— but he also knew that it was the right thing to do. If he'd not been prodded by her to take such action, she wasn't sure if he'd go that far or not. But he was now, and she was quite sure it was not only do the right thing but to appease her as well.

She watched him speak to one of the women behind the desk. The woman smiled brightly and the two of them chuckled about something. Frank then leaned in a little closer and spoke secretively to her. The woman nodded, looked down to something hidden behind the desk, and responded. Frank gave her a smile, drummed his fingers on top of the desk and turned back around.

He met Ava's gaze and gave her a little nod as he gestured her over.

Apparently, Duggar was indeed on patrol.

And they were yet again heading back to that same part of town.

CHAPTER TWENTY SEVEN

"The question I have," Ava said as they started patrolling the streets of the Lower East Side yet again, "is why Duggar would be sent out here at all. If the precinct or the entire police force at large isn't taking immigrant crime seriously, why waste someone like Duggar—a man that is apparently known for getting the job done."

"My guess is that he requested it," Franks said "If he really feels so strongly about illegal immigrants, maybe he figures being in the thick of it will give him more opportunity to make some arrests. Looks good on his record and he becomes known for standing for a very specific cause." He shrugged and added: "I don't agree with his beliefs, but it's a damned smart move."

They were three blocks away from where Edith Lange had been killed just two hours ago. Dusk had not yet quite fallen, but it was in the air. Most patrols would end around five or six in the afternoon, depending on the officer's shift. If it was five for Duggar, there was a very good chance he may already be on the way back to the station. Ava's hope was that he would have a car at his disposal and spend as much time on the streets as he could.

It took them about five minutes of walking before they saw their first cop. It was a tall man in a well-pressed uniform, standing on the corner and allowing an elderly woman to pass before a stream of autos went crossing the intersection.

"Is that him?" Ava asked.

"No. Duggar isn't very tall. Probably about my height. And he has a beard on him that will make you think of a Civil War general. You really can't miss him."

The streets were quite crowded now. There were a few people peddling various wares—from pocket watches to hats. Some people were coming in from work for the day while others were starting to head out for a night of revelry. Alcohol may be illegal, but people still found a way to have a good time.

It was a bit rowdier out here than what Ava was accustomed to. Any police officer that voluntarily took this beat either loved the area or likely had some sort of hidden agenda—like Duggar, apparently.

Ava looked down each and every alley they passed, feeling as if she were stuck on a never-ending loop. It was hard to think that they'd only been investigating this part of town for two days; it was starting to feel much longer. Some of the alleys were partially blocked off by broken boards, bits of chipped brick and other remnants of failed construction. Others were clogged with garbage. Here and there, they came across one that was mostly open, carbon copies of the sort that Eve and Edith had been murdered in. There was some activity in these, but it was mostly just immigrants huddled together: women doing laundry, kids at play, and men huddled together to speak quietly.

Just as Ava was sure they were going to end up going back to the precinct with nothing more than plans to look into William Duggar tomorrow, she heard a commotion coming from an alleyway just ahead of them. They were now about seven blocks away from where Edith had been killed—about five blocks away from where the streets and buildings started to look slightly more evolved.

She looked over to Frank and saw that he had heard it, too. His eyes scanned to the left as they hurried to the alleyway. Ava heard something falling over, clattering to the ground with the sound of wood and scraping glass. When they reached the alleyway and looked into it, Ava felt like she was looking back into the past. The scene was eerily similar to the moment they'd first found Harvey Jackson. Here, in this alley, was another man bullying an immigrant woman. The shocking difference between the two scenes, though, was that this man was wearing a police uniform. And the very bushy beard that Frank had mentioned earlier was hard to miss.

"That's Duggar," Frank said, easing his way into the alley.

Ava didn't quite have the same restraint that Frank was showing. She walked with quick steps at first but then when she saw Duggar—a man of at least one hundred and seventy pounds—shoving a woman that might weigh about one hundred, she hurried her step.

Behind her, Frank called out to Duggar, perhaps already fully aware of what was going to happen.

"Hey, Duggar!"

But even then, it was just a bit too late. Duggar turned towards Frank's voice and when he did, Ava was already there. It took a great deal of effort not to punch the miserable son of a bitch in the jaw. Instead, she simply shoved both of her arms out, her palms striking him solidly in the chest. Not expecting this at all, Duggar let out a shout of surprise and stumbled backwards. His feet tangled and he went to the ground hard on his backside.

The look of fury and embarrassment that came across his face made Ava panic just the slightest bit. But as he scrambled to his feet, she found that she'd already slipped into an offensive boxing stance, her fists clenched and ready.

"What the hell do you think you're doing?" he screamed. He came charging at her but then saw Frank. And seeing Frank, Duggar seemed to understand what was going on.

"Ava Gold," he said, snickering. He then sneered at Frank, shaking his head. "Wimbly, you might want to get this daffy dame in check before I knock her fucking lights out."

"I don't think it'll come to that," Frank said.

"Why are you two interfering with my investigation?" Duggar asked.

"What investigation?" Ava asked. "Seems to me you were only beating up on a woman. A very small, defenseless woman, at that."

The woman remained pinned against the wall, trapped on her right by Duggar and on her left by Ava and Frank. As Ava stared Duggar down, Frank stepped aside and gestured for the woman to make her way out of the alley. She did, and quickly, letting out a series of whimpers that trailed behind her.

"She was an illegal," Duggar growled. "And you just let her go."

"You'd prefer we rough her up a bit?" Ava asked.

"Someone needs to enforce the law around here."

"That's why we're here," Frank said, stepping closer. "Duggar, I don't know if you're aware of it or not, but Detective Gold and I are working a homicide case."

"Oh, I know why you're here. Everyone at the precinct thinks you're wasting your time trying to solve the murder of some poor immigrant woman."

"Two women," Frank corrected him. "There was another one earlier this afternoon."

"Is that so?"

Ava didn't like the attitude coming off of Duggar. It was clear that he thought he was superior to both of them and that he saw nothing wrong with what he was doing. If they were going to get honest answers out of him about what he'd been up to lately, it was going to be much more difficult than she'd been expecting.

Duggar eyed them suspiciously as a thick silence nestled in between them. "Do I see and hear some accusation coming from the two of you?"

"No," Frank said. "But we *would* like to know more about what your patrols are like. With all due respect, you have been on more patrols out here than anyone else over the past month or so. And given that there have been two deaths and at least one attempted assault that we know about, it makes me wonder how your constant presence hasn't prevented things like that."

"Still sounds like an accusation," Duggar said. "And quite frankly, I don't appreciate it."

"Maybe," Ava said, unable to help herself, "it sounds like an accusation because you feel guilty."

Duggar stepped forward, looking down at her. He had at least five inches and forty pounds on her and though she'd stepped up to men a bit bigger in a boxing ring, this was different. She tried to remind herself of that as she took a matching step forward, the two of them now standing less than a foot apart.

"Stand down, Duggar," Frank said. "And Av—Gold, turn away."

Duggar nodded slowly. "Yeah, I'll stand down. She's not worth it. Sticking her nose in problems like this to make herself look bigger." He took his step back, creating more space between them. "Seems like she might be compensating for something. Maybe trying too hard to fill her dead husband's shoes. Shouldn't be too hard. He was fucking soft, too."

The comment was like a stab to her heart. It took infinite restraint to keep from punching him. He turned his back and started walking back down the alley, maybe to go find and terrorize more immigrants.

"Stop," Ava said. "We have questions for you."

"Yeah, like what?" Duggar stopped but didn't turn to face her.

"Like why you insist on trying to wrangle in illegals. Like why you were right here, in the neighborhood, when a woman was killed a few hours ago. I think it was you, Duggar. I think you killed them and—"

Duggar turned quickly. When he did, he brought his right arm around in a wild haymaker. If he'd been just a bit faster, his fist would have collided with Ava's face and very likely shattered her cheek. But thanks to her boxing training, Ava was quick on her feet and saw the punch coming before she even saw his fist. She pivoted back just a half step. Even then, the punch was close—so close that she felt the wind of it as it passed by her face.

When it went zipping past, she reached out and grabbed him by the elbow with her right hand. She pushed that hand hard in an upward motion, causing Duggar to stumble forward. When he did, she used her left hand to punch him in the back, shoving him hard into the brick wall to her right.

She knew right away that she'd put a bit too much force into it. This was proven by the sickening cracking noise as Duggar's face slammed into the wall. He yelped out in pain and the combination of the noises, and her sudden outburst of action caused Ava to release him and take a step back.

"Jesus, Ava," Frank said, rushing forward. "What are y—"

Duggar turned in a half-circle away from the wall, throwing his right elbow out. It clipped Ava in the chin and sent her stumbling backwards. He then came at her in a charge, his shoulder hunched and his head lowered. Still dazed, she realized the idiocy of his attack right away and put a stop to it by simply raising her knee in a quick motion. It connected with Duggar's forehead, sending him to the ground. Ava started to topple, too, but caught herself against the wall.

Frank stood dumbfounded between both of them. Ava was a bit light-headed and gave him a nod, indicating that she was okay. Frank ran a nervous hand through his hair as he sized up the situation. He walked over to Duggar and knelt down beside him. Duggar was slowly rolling over onto his back, groaning.

"Duggar," Frank said. "Did you do it? Did you kill those women?"

There was silence for a moment, and then Duggar spit in Frank's face. It was tinged with blood. More than that, Ava saw that a tooth also came out.

Frank furiously wiped the spit away and let out a very heavy sigh. Then, uttering a curse, he reached into his inside coat pocket an took out his handcuffs. And when he started to snap them around Duggar's wrists, Duggar didn't even try to resist.

CHAPTER TWENTY EIGHT

Ava had been expecting a bit of backlash when she and Frank came into the precinct with yet another police officer handcuffed. She understood it; given the cases she'd been assigned lately it was becoming something of a routine with her. What she had not expected, though, was the level of backlash. Even Frank seemed taken aback by it as they walked into the precinct with Duggar handcuffed between them.

It started the moment the three of them were past the front desk and nearing the bullpen. It started as whispers—some hushed *oh my God*s and *You seeing this?* But then it got much more vocal and Ava wondered if she had finally stepped a bit too far over the line.

"Are you kidding me?" one officer said, getting to his feet.

"Gold! *Wimbly!* What do you think you're doing?" The man that made this comment stalked directly to Minard's office and made no attempt to hide that he was about to knock on the door and discuss this with the Captain.

And all the while, Duggar smiled between them. Even when he was shoved into a chair in an interrogation room less than a minute later, his busted lips were smiling. He was bleeding from the brow, had gotten a tooth knocked out, had busted his lips up, and the end of his nose had been scratched open against the brick wall. But the bastard was still *smiling.*

"Something funny?" Frank asked him.

"Very funny. Gold, do you really want to lose this job? You don't have any friends out there. You saw that, right?"

"I didn't take this job to make me friends."

"Oh, I know. You did it because of your dead hu—"

Frank slammed his hands down on the table, making both Duggar and Ava jump. "Mention Clarence Gold again and I'll be the one to knock you down next time. Got it?"

Duggar clammed up, but the smile was still on his face. As Ava studied him and tried to think of where to even start the line of questioning, she could hear a commotion outside of the interrogation door. So far, though, no one dared to open it.

"Two women have been murdered over the last three days in an area of the city you have knowingly been patrolling," Ava said. "Tie that up with the fact that you've also arrested several of them, even bringing some in beaten and bloodied, and it paints a decent picture. If you were a cop worth a damn, you'd understand why we came to talk to you. Eve Buzek and Edith Lange. Both dead. Did you approach them and demand to see their papers?"

"I don't ask for the names," he said, licking drying blood from his lips. "And of course I did not *kill* people. Do I think some of those lousy immigrants deserve it? Maybe…yeah, maybe so. But I'm a cop, you idiots. Of course I wouldn't *kill them!"*

"Do you happen to recall where you were today around—"

"I'm not answering these questions. I'm going to sit here like a good boy that was wrongly attacked and wait for Minard to show up and nail your asses to the wall. Gold…you and so-called dirty cops. It's ridiculous and everyone hates you. No one trusts you and more than half of the cops out there in that station would go out of their way to *not* help you. 134as that your goal from the start? Was that…"

He stopped here, maybe sensing that he might say something incriminating. He shrugged and stared them both down.

"I don't get it," Frank said. "All you have to do is tell us where you were at a certain time today and three days ago. Why is that a problem?"

"Because I'm not a criminal."

"But if you—"

The door opened quickly, cutting him off. Captain Minard stood there with a stoic expression on his face, but Ava could see the frustration lurking behind it. A few others lurked behind him and as he stepped into the interrogation room, he looked back to them.

"Back to your desks!" he yelled. He then stepped directly to the table in the interrogation room and looked at all three of them. Ava could see that he was trying to think of the best way to play this and for a moment, she understood that she could very well be on the verge of losing her job.

"Wimbly," Minard said. "Would you take Officer Duggar to the next interrogation room over?"

"Yes, sir."

"Office Duggar, please answer any questions Detective Wimbly has. Let's not make this any worse and tackier than it already is. I'll speak to each of you individually after this is over but for right now, please just answer his questions."

"Yes, sir." It was extremely clear that he did not like this suggestion at all.

Frank helped Duggar up out of the chair and marched him to the door. When they were out, Minard closed the door behind them. When he turned to look at Ava, she could not tell what he was thinking. There was no real emotion on his face, none that she could clearly read, anyway.

"You went after Duggar?"

"We went to question him, yes."

"On what grounds?"

"He's been on patrols on the Lower East Side constantly over the past few weeks. And I have it on good authority that on at least one occasion, he brought in immigrants that he'd assaulted. The fact that he was in the area today when a woman was murdered was suspicious to me—not to mention the same thing happened three days ago, while he was on patrol in the area."

"Do you have proof?"

It felt like a punch to the gut because no, she did not. "No, sir."

"Why is he bleeding right now?"

"We found him assaulting an immigrant woman in an alleyway. He was getting very rough with her. So Detective Wimbly and I stepped in to stop him. The discussion got heated and he took a swing at me."

She wasn't sure how to feel that Minard did not look surprised at this—or the fact that despite Duggar's swing, he was the one that had come in bleeding and bruised.

"Here's the thing, Gold. I've gotten a few complaints about Duggar over the past six months. Nothing that would land him any criminal charges, but enough for me to keep an eye on him. As for these immigrant arrests he's been making, they're all legitimate. But, you know about the Undesirable Aliens Act, right?"

"Yes, sir. It states that when you illegally enter the US, it is treated as a misdemeanor and can result in up to a year in prison."

"That's right. And he's brought in eight in the past five weeks. So while he may be a bit rough in his approach, he's showing results. His results and those complaints I've gotten against him sort of butt heads, you see. But I need to ask you right now, just you and I here alone, if you think the man is capable of murder."

"I don't know him well enough to make that call," Ava admitted. "I was going on the little bit of evidence I had. And based on things you've just told me, I feel even more confident in deciding to question him." She hesitated here and then, fearing it might be a bit of an overstep on her part, asked: "What about you, sir?"

"What do you mean?"

"You know Duggar much better than I do. Do you think he's capable of murder?"

Minard rubbed at his head, looking like he was doing his best to push an oncoming headache away. "I don't know. When that law was passed, he took it as a mission of sorts. He's dedicated, that's for sure, but the complaints are based on violent behavior." He sighed and shook his head. "You say he took the first swing?"

"Yes, sir."

"Wimbly will back that up?"

She nodded. She couldn't help but wonder if he suspected the blossoming romance between her and Frank. "Yes, sir. He also did his best to prod me into taking the first swing. He spoke ill about Clarence."

"I see." He stood silently for a good twenty seconds, thinking things over. While Ava felt a bit more confident that she wasn't about to be fired, she still felt quite uneasy. "I'm going to ask you to stay here, in this room for a while. Quite a while, actually. But that's only because I'm going to have Duggar stay a while, too. I'll talk to him, see if I can figure out if there's any real reason to hold him on suspicion of murder. But as far as anyone outside knows, I'm just dealing with some in-fighting within the department. I have to make it look as good as I can for you, Gold. You're not making any friends out there, you know?"

"Yes, I know. Duggar made that clear. Sorry, sir." "No need to apologize," he said, though he did seem slightly frustrated. "You're doing good work and making calls most other cops would make. You just…you need to have a better filter about how you approach cases that might reach its fingers into the department."

With that comment, he made his exit. The room went quiet, and she could just barely make out the sound of Minard going into the neighboring interrogation room.

She sat in the silence for a moment, coming to the understanding that Minard seemed to be firmly on her side. Whether that was because he was still cheering on the female detective that had earned the force so many positive headlines and attention, she didn't know. 136ut for now, she figured she'd take what she could get.

A few minutes later, the door opened again, and Frank stepped inside. He sat down in the chair behind the table and crossed his arms. "Well, if he *did* do it, there's no way he's coming clean. And I don't know that Minard is going to send any sort of serious investigation out into those alleys to see if he can prove that one of his officers is guilty of killing two women when there isn't much evidence to support it."

"I don't know," she said, running her previous conversation with Minard through her head. "I think you might be surprised by what he'd be willing to do. Apparently, he's gotten lots of complaints about Duggar recently."

"I figured as much. But still…no matter how this ends up, I don't see this going well for you. You're really rubbing people the wrong way. People on the force, anyway. The public still seems to like you."

"Hey, I'll take what I can get."

"Good," he said, shooting her a smile. "If it helps, I kind of like you, too."

"It does, a bit."

"You ready to call it a day?"

"I can't," she said. She then explained Minard's plans to him, letting him know she'd be spending the next hour or two (or more, for all she knew) in this room. "So if you would, I would really appreciate it if you could call the apartment and let my dad and Jeffrey know what's going on."

"Yeah, I can do that." He headed for the door and turned to her one last time before heading out. "When you took the job, did you ever think you'd be sitting in one of these rooms not to interrogate, but as a form of punishment?"

She smiled right back and said, "You know, I think I did."

Ava watched Frank leave, closing the door behind him, to let her family know that it might be a while before she was going to get home—that it was looking to be a long night.

CHAPTER TWENTY NINE

The door opened just as Ava was looking to her watch. It was 8:10 at night. Minard had held her for a little over two hours. When she glanced up to the door, Minard stood there, looking tired and irritated.

"You're free to go," he said.

She got to her feet and looked to the wall to her right. "And him?"

Minard went back to rubbing at his head again. Ava wondered if he kept a chronic headache, given the stress of his job. "I'm keeping him a bit longer. I'm pretty certain he didn't kill anyone, but the deeper I look and the more officers I speak to, there's something there for sure. And I'll be damned if I'm going to let one of my men participate in criminal activity and then try to hide behind the badge as a defense." He studied her for a moment, as if trying to deice if he should say more. He turned for the door and looked back over his shoulder. "I'm not going to give you the details but because of your actions today, you may have uncovered a few things about underhanded dealings Duggar has been involved in—abuse against immigrants being only part of it. So we're going to hold him indefinitely. And that's going to be a blow to how everyone around here sees you."

"Thanks for trusting my judgement," Ava said, surprised how moved she was to feel that Minard had her back.

"It's not solely about your judgement, Gold. You just seem to have a knack for poking your nose into messes that have been caused by fellow police officers. That's not judgement at all; I'd call that bad luck."

He left her alone in the room again, only this time, the difference was that she could leave right behind him. She did that very thing, finding herself suddenly anxious to be with her son.

***

Jeffrey was asleep when she got home, so Ava settled for laying down with him and spooning him. He seemed to sense his mother's presence and curled into her for a moment. He was a reminder of why she had the job. A reminder of why she needed to stick it out and not give up just because doing the right thing was making a few cops mad.

She kissed his forehead and quietly scooted out of bed. She found her father still sitting in the small den. He had fallen asleep in the armchair, the day's paper draped over his knee. She thought it was a bit early to pass out in such a way but then again, he was fifty-six years old and ran a boxing gym.

Ava allowed herself to enjoy a warm bath and let her mind go blank for a while. She massaged her chin where Duggar had gotten in a pretty good shot with his elbow. It had swollen some, but the pain was minimal. She found herself thinking of Frank and wishing he were there—not in the tub with her, but maybe waiting at the kitchen table so she could have an ear to talk to. She wasn't naive enough to think that she was in love with him yet but she was beginning to understand that he was quickly becoming an integral part of her life. She missed him when he was not there and was relying on him for safety and security in places other than the police force.

She retired to bed half an hour later, certain that the next day would be rife with hostility and intrusive questioning by others on the force. She also couldn't help but wonder what would become of Duggar. She couldn't help but feel a little selfish in thinking that her immediate future would end up being much easier if Duggar was charged with something. If he was let go and she had to work in the same precinct as him after what had happened between them, she saw nothing but conflict on the horizon.

Even with these thoughts plaguing her head, she was able to fall asleep relatively easily. But it wasn't too long before her mind was filled with fragmented dreams—dreams of seedy alleyways where women were dying, dropping like flies and piling up between buildings as if they were nothing more than piles of rotten, discarded garbage.

She woke up at one point, heart hammering in her chest as she rubbed habitually at her neck. For a moment, she felt certain someone was choking her.

She looked around her dark bedroom and realized that she could hear a soft and delicate noise coming from elsewhere in the apartment. She sat up at the edge of the bed, listening closely. She glanced at her watch in the gloom of her room and saw that it was 3:40 in the morning Still, she was pretty sure she heard the kettle moving on the stove and the clink of a coffee cup on the counter.

Curious, she got up and made her way out of her room, into the kitchen. Blurry eyed, she found her father waiting for the kettle to boil. She saw that he'd placed a tea bag into his favorite mug.

"What're you doing up?" Ava asked.

Roosevelt shook his head, frowning. "Didn't mean to wake you. Sorry. I've got this bladder thing. Dunno if it's irritated or something more serious, but it's been bothering me for weeks now. Sometimes it gets me up on the middle of the night. Tonight, I gave up on going back to sleep."

"You put enough water in for two cups?"

"There might be enough, yeah. But shouldn't you go back to sleep?"

"Probably," she said, getting out a mug.

They stood in silence until the kettle whistled. Pouring the water into his cup, Roosevelt said, "You have a rough day?"

"Yeah, it was a bit much. But tomorrow may be even harder."

"Want to talk it out?"

She considered it but shook her head. "Not all of it, no. I've just…over the past few days, I've gotten a really good glimpse into the life of some of the less fortunate immigrants living in this city. I see how they're treated, how they have to live to get by."

"They have you looking into illegals?"

"No, not really. We're working a murder case and I'm finding that there's a whole group of people out there that don't trust the police. I'm also finding that they have good reason not to. No one is helping them. People only see them as legal or illegal."

Roosevelt sipped from his tea with a small frown on his face. "Yeah, I'm guilty of that myself. I understand that there are rules that have to be followed to live here, but the way some of the illegals are treated…it's pretty bad."

"I want to help them, but some of these immigrants are—"

"Can I say something?"

"Of course."

"I'm no detective and honestly, I think you'd probably disagree with some of my deeper political opinions. But maybe you'd have an easier time relating to them if you stopped referring to them as immigrants. They're people, just like me and you. They just happen to have come from somewhere else, hoping to find a better life here. I mean, how are they different from you and I other than the fact that when they arrived here, they had to start from the very bottom? They're real people with real problems—real jobs, real families and real problems."

Ava almost responded to this immediately, but the words caught in her throat. *My God, he's right,* she thought. *I may not loathe them like the William Duggars of the world, but by putting them in a box labelled "immigrant" am I really that much better?*

"See?" Roosevelt said. "I spoke out of turn, didn't I?"

"No, not at all," she said, the revelation starting to form another piece to the case in her mind. "I just…well, I didn't know you cared that much about the immigrant cause."

"I don't really think I do, but I've always not liked it when a certain group of people are looked down on. Humans are humans—I don't care where you come from or what you're struggling with. Who the hell am I to criticize someone for their upbringing?"

Ava smiled, not only proud of this surprising revelation from her father, but at how it was helping her to sort some elements of the case out in her head. She started to wonder how the case and the leads may have shaped up differently if she'd viewed the victims as *people* first, rather than immigrants. What if, for example, they weren't being targeted because they were immigrants? If she took the label of immigrant away, how would she have approached the case differently?

She was actually rather ashamed that she'd made such a mistake. She'd allowed herself to see the victims as the rest of the world saw them—as something different than so-called *normal* people.

So she brought the most pressing question to the front of her mind: How would she and Frank have approached the case if Eve Buzek and Edith Lange had not been immigrants?

She knew answer and she wanted to act right away. But being nearly four in the morning, she still had a few hours to wait before she could act. In the meantime, she could just enjoy this cup of tea with her father. And then, after trying to nab a few more hours of sleep, she'd spend the morning with her son before heading off to work.

It was undoubtedly going to be a tough day, but she was starting to wonder if she might be able to start it off in a way that might make up for the rest.

CHAPTER THIRTY

Ava walked Jeffrey to school a bit earlier than normal. She'd decided at some point before drifting back off to sleep that she wasn't going to head to the precinct right away after taking Jeffrey to school. If she did that, she'd get caught up in the drama of what had happened to Duggar. And while she was anxious to know the outcome there, she did not see the point in getting mired down in conversations with Minard. And, if she was being honest with herself, she wanted to stave off the scrutiny and angry glances and remarks she was sure to receive from the bullpen.

She did her usual thing, standing on the street and watching Jeffrey until he disappeared through the doors of the school. She then walked a few blocks closer to the precinct and stopped when she saw an available cab parked on the side of the street. She slid into the back and the driver greeted her with a practiced smile.

"Where to, ma'am?" he asked in a flirty tone.

"The Garment District, please."

The driver pulled out into traffic and headed north. Ava started to feel guilty for not going to the station first, mostly because she hated the idea of going somewhere behind Frank's back. She was quite sure he would have come along with her and hoped he wouldn't think she was being tricky. At the end of the day, though, he knew her well and she thought he would understand.

Traffic wasn't too bad, though the initial clog of the morning bustle slowed them a bit. It was nearing nine o'clock when Ava paid the driver and stepped out of the cab. She thought of the little jab Wanda had made when they had come to visit her a second time, something along the lines of how the cops were just going to keep harassing her until they found the answers to the poor, dead immigrant's murder. And now here she was yet again to ask even more questions.

When she stepped inside the warehouse, she saw Wanda right away. She was not out on the work floor, hidden behind the walls beyond the lobby and waiting area. This morning, she was helping two other women behind the front counter as they cut away very carefully measured strips of fabric. The helpful and polite owner Ava and Frank had spoken to on earlier occasions was talking with a delivery driver off to the side, both men looking at a clipboard.

Wanda looked up and saw Ava right away. A look of irritation crossed her face as she continued to measure out the strips of fabric. Ava approached the front desk and gave Wanda an apologetic look.

"I know. It's a little ridiculous that I'm back. But you have my word that this is the last time."

At first, Wanda said nothing. She doled out another length of fabric for one of the other women to cut and then made her way around the desk. "What is it now?" she asked.

"I'm trying a different approach this time around," Ava said. "I'm wondering what things are like where you live. An old neighbor of yours told me and my partner that you're currently in an apartment with two other ladies—that you were able to move out of the tenements."

"Yes, that's right. We can just barely afford it, but we've made it work."

"Do you have family here?"

"A sister. My father came, too. But he died on the boat on the way over."

"To afford an apartment so soon after getting here…I take it you get paid well here?"

"It's decent. It's certainly better than the place I worked before."

"And where was that?"

"A textile mill really close to where I used to live. That dark, brick one over on Packer Street."

"And how long did you work there?"

"I don't know. Maybe two weeks. The pay was just horrendous and the guy we were working for was an absolute madman. Didn't give us breaks. My sister heard about this place," she said, gesturing all around here, "and here I am."

Ava almost started asking another question but then realized that something Wanda said triggered a small memory in her head. She pulled up the facts she'd memorized regarding the case, going over everything she'd learned about the victims.

Eve Buzek. What about her? Ava thought of the tall woman at the laundry Eve had worked at. She'd said something about Eve coming from another job where she'd been unhappy, where the employer was taking advantage of the immigrants' need for employment.

It had been at a textile mill. And it had been with an owner just like the one Wanda was describing. A miserable man that ran his employees ragged. Especially immigrant women.

"You said you worked there for two weeks? The textile mill?"

"Yeah. Got out of there as quickly as I could."

"How long ago was this?"

"Not sure. Maybe two months."

"And you never met a woman named Eve Buzek that worked there?"

"No. But if she did work there, that doesn't mean I would have ever met her. People came and went all the time, swapping shifts and stations." She eyed Ava with an almost excited curiosity. "Why? You think she might have worked there?"

The memory came clearer, the laundry owner talking about how she came to know Eve.

"She was so happy to find work here...she had previously worked at a textile mill, and they were paying her terribly. No breaks, twelve hour shifts six days a week..."

It was definitely worth looking into. And though she knew it was something she should collaborate with Frank on, she also had no interest in getting held up at the precinct. She was pretty sure people would start to notice her absence soon—particularly Frank and Minard—so she figured she could stretch out the morning a bit more. She was already going to get lectured about not showing up on a tense morning; what was the harm in getting in just a bit more trouble?

"Over on Packer Street, you said?" Ava asked.

"Yeah. Looks like the place might collapse at any minute. You can't miss it."

"Thank you," Ava said, heading for the door. "And don't worry, Wanda. I can promise you this time that you won't see me again."

It was a promise Ava intended to keep as she hurried out of the warehouse with a new lead ahead of her—a lead that was taking her back, yet again, to where so many immigrants had been forced to live in squalor while waiting for their dreams to take form.

***

Wanda had not been joking around. The mill reminded Ava of something she'd once read out of one of Edgar Alan Poe's tales. It was chipped and scarred, like something that has survived a fire that had never happened. It was the type of building that would likely spark tales of ghosts and demons. Perhaps the saddest thing of all was that it did not look all that different from some of the other buildings on Packer Street and the neighboring area.

She could find no front entrance as she walked through the thin parade of morning pedestrians. It took walking down an alley between the building and its decrepit neighbor for her to find a way inside. She tried the small, wooden door but found it locked. She leaned closer to the door and heard the very clear sounds of machinery operating inside.

Ava knocked on the door, wasting no time with soft raps. She knocked as if trying to knock the door down, a series of rapid-fire whacks that drew the attention of a few passersby on the street. After about thirty seconds, the door was opened. It opened only halfway, revealing a blonde woman of about Ava's age. She was coated in sweat and her face had streaks of dirt and grime along her cheeks and jaw.

"Hello?" the woman asked.

"Hello. This is the textile mill, yes?"

The woman looked confused at first but slowly nodded. "Yes, this is a textile mill."

Ava showed her badge and, without being invited, stepped forward. "I need to come inside."

The woman started to protest, pushing her scrawny frame against the door. Ava didn't even have to push all that hard to get in. The woman tottered back, looking at Ava as if she were a monster.

"Is your supervisor here?" Ava asked.

"No ma'am, he's not."

Ava tucked her badge away and took her first good look at the place. It was mostly one big, open floor. The only wall of any kind she could see was farther off in the back, giving way to a few small offices. But the rest of the place was nothing more than a concrete floor. About a dozen large machines were bolted to the floor. Most of them were churning out raw strands of yarn and other fabrics into spools. Each machine was attended by three to five women, some catching the material off the back end while others fed it into the machine and made sure it stayed on track.

Right away, Ava noticed that the vast majority of the workers were women. A few men were thrown in here and there, just as scrawny as the women that were working the machines. Ava looked back to the woman who had answered the door and saw that she still looked terrified.

"I'm not here looking for illegals," she said. She had to raise her voice slightly to be heard over the humming and thrumming of the machines. "I truly only need to speak to your supervisor."

The blonde woman looked to the floor, giving her head a quick shake. Ava noticed that a few others had noticed her presence. Several women and one man watched what was transpiring from their stations behind the machines.

"Listen to me," Ava said to the blonde woman. "Do you know women by the name of Eve Buzek or Edith Lange?"

At the mention of Edith's name, the woman looked up. She didn't look at Ava, but across the room. Her eyes fell on one of the women working the machines. This woman, a short and strikingly beautiful redhead, was looking right back. Sensing something there, some hidden secret perhaps, Ava marched across the floor. The redhead looked like a deer caught in a hunter's stare. She backed away from the machine a few steps, already shaking her head.

"What is it?" Ava asked, suddenly feeling as if *she* were the one doing something wrong. "I just have questions about a few women that worked here."

"Ma'am," the blonde said, catching up to her. "We've been told to never talk to the police. We could lose our jobs."

"Okay, so everyone listen to me," Ava shouted, her voice rising over the machines. "I am not here to arrest any illegals. I am not interested in your papers or your legal status. Right now, I am investigating the murders of two women I believe once worked here. Their names are Eve Buzek and Edith Lange."

The redhead gasped, a hand going to her mouth. "Edith?" she said from behind her hand.

"Yes. And I'm sorry to break the news to you in such a way. But no one wants to talk to the cops—it's not just you." She eyed the workers and saw that even the men looked aghast at what she was saying. "They both worked here, correct?"

She got several nods and a murmured *"yes"* from the redhead—apparently a friend of Edith's. She then stepped forward with tears in her eyes. "Edith…she worked here for about ten days. That's all. She was desperate for the money. She was…my God, she was having to eat rats from the street before this. She…she…"

Ava looked back to the blonde. She seemed to have come around a bit now that everyone was more or less involved in the conversation. "Where is your supervisor?"

"Like I said, he's not here."

"He's hardly ever here," said another of the women, this one with a very rich Italian accent.

She nodded, not liking what this meant. Without the help of a supervisor, she was going to have to rely on the word of these scared immigrants. "What's his name?"

No one answered right away, but the redhead finally got it out, her voice still wavering with the news of her friend's death. "Ted Johnson."

Ava thought about her options from this point, feeling that the case was suddenly presenting itself right before her. A few well-thought-out questions and she might have this damn thing solved.

"I need to know when this shift started," Ava said.

"Eight o' clock this morning," said the blonde.

Ava checked her watch and saw that it was now nearing ten. "And did anyone not show up for work this morning?"

One of the men answered this. Based on his expression of interest and somewhat conspiratorial tone, Ava thought he might have picked up on what she was trying to figure out. But even then, as she handled the disappointment of the supervisor not being there, she was struck with another idea—an idea that grew quite large as this man spoke to her.

"Gina. She showed up and worked for about fifteen minutes but then had to leave. She has terrible headaches from time to time and she just couldn't stand it this morning."

"And the supervisor let her go?"

"Yeah," the blonde said. "He wasn't happy about it, but he let her go."

It all started to click, the pieces aligning in Ava's head. Two women dead, both having worked at this mill at some point. A supervisor that had a reputation for being rather brutal and uncaring— the same supervisor that was currently not at his place of business at the same time a vulnerable, immigrant woman was also missing.

A new spark of worry flared in her stomach. "This is very important," she said, eyeing every one of the workers. "Does *anyone* happen to know where Gina lives?"

"I do," another woman said. Her voice was soft and meek, almost completely drowned out by the roaring of the machines. "It's a small building on Burbank Avenue. One of those two story deals that looks like it's about to fall over. Boards on the windows. It's right where the—"

But Ava was already rushing back for the door. She knew exactly where it was—mainly because she and Frank had passed it at least three times in the past day or so. It was, in fact, less than two blocks away from here this had started started, where the body of Eve Buzek had been found.

She raced back to the cab, gave him the address, and sat back in the seat. She now had a fairly strong lead; she even had his name but had no idea what he looked like. And because she'd rushed into this so fast, she'd be going it alone.

Ava thought of Frank, and then of the two dead women and realized there was no way she could have waited. She was more confident than ever that the killer was out there, stalking a new victim, and that it would now come down to a race between her and a killer that seemed to be getting braver and more confident with each strike.

CHAPTER THIRTY ONE

One thing he'd never been certain of was whether the women he kept in his employ were just scared of him or flat out stupid. So far, none of them seemed to have noticed what he was up to. When he's first started knocking them off, he feared it would be hard to cover his tracks, especially after bumbling the attempt with Wanda on Ellis Isle.

But the broads had never even suspected him. So far, this whole thing had been duck soup. Even the cops weren't onto him, mainly because they didn't seem to care very much about crimes committed against immigrants. In other words, they had the same mindset towards them as he did.

Still, he knew what he was doing was wrong. It's why he was currently keeping his eyes peeled for coppers and dicks as he made his way to Burbank Avenue. Gina was about fifteen minutes ahead of him, probably already in that ramshackle dump she called a home. He knew where she lived because he'd followed here there several times. He'd followed her, watching her backside twitch, imagining what it would feel like in his hands, what her tongue might taste like when he pressed her hard against one of these grimy brick walls.

He'd not even approached Gina with any interest yet. He'd been rejected by enough of them and it was starting to hurt. Yes, he'd had his way with a few of them. It's how some of these daft immigrant women had gotten jobs with him. Some still serviced him regularly just to make sure they could keep the job. It was a pretty good deal.

But he wanted more. Gina was something special. He could just look at Gina and tell that she was going to reject him. It was something in her eyes, the same sort of defiance he'd seen in Edith Lange's eyes when she'd drawn back and slapped him when he'd pulled her to the side after a shift and cupped her breast.

He didn't get it. He didn't understand how some of them were so subservient and almost seemed *pleased* to offer themselves as a means of job security. Shouldn't all of these broads be grateful for an American man to be interested in them? It meant security and safety. It meant not having to scrounge for food and to know they wouldn't be forever sleeping in the alleys or those shady tenements.

He supposed it was his reaction to this mindset that had caused him to start killing them. He'd come to find that murder was a thrill unlike any other. While he did enjoy the romps he had with the more vulnerable ones from time to time, taking their lives was something totally different. A different sort of control. A different way to make them his.

Approaching Burbank Avenue, he reached into his coat pocket and felt the scarf—the same scarf that had once been worn around his wife' neck. A wife that had come from Scandinavia and had treated him like a king. God, but he'd loved that woman, his precious Mia. She'd died with this scarf around her neck, a slow death from a disease she'd brought from her homeland.

He understood the direction of his anger. He understood that it had started by looking for an immigrant woman like Mia, a woman needing the security and safety of a local man. But no one had ever compared. No one had ever matched Mia's unyielding love and need for his strong hand and safety. And while he knew that sleeping with his workers and killing all immigrant women that rejected hm would never bring Mia back, it did ease the pain a bit.

And there was another in his sights. Gina's building was there, just up ahead, one of many buildings just like it over the next several blocks. These buildings, all lined up so ghastly and symmetrical may as well have been a cemetery—each building a grave plot for his next victim.

He smirked as he came to the building. Still gripping Mia's scarf in his pocket, he turned down the alley beside the building and waited for the right moment.

CHAPTER THIRTY TWO

Ava realized her mistake when she came to the block she'd had in mind. For a stretch of about two blocks, all of the buildings looked almost identical. They were all deteriorating, most of them were two-stories, and over half of them had at least one or two windows that had been boarded over. As she looked to the first building and realized her error, she cursed under her breath—one of the really bad ones that Clarence used to blush at when he heard it come out of her mouth.

Knowing that she had no other option, she ran to the first door and knocked. She knocked the same way she had when she'd approached the textile mill, essentially punching the door. Even in doing this, she knew it might be useless. If the supervisor—Ted Johnson—had already struck and there was no one else home, there would be no one to answer. There could be a dead woman on the other side of the door and she wouldn't know it.

She found herself resisting the urge to shout through the door, to let anyone that may be hiding on the other side that she was with the police. If Johnson hadn't struck yet, that would be a surefire way to get him to run and she'd never know.

Giving up on the first door, she came to another. When she knocked on this one with her heavy hand, she was shocked when it opened up right away. Inside, she was surprised what she saw. This was not one of the decrepit open-floor dwellings, but an actual attempt at some sort of apartment building. The very small lobby gave way to five apartments along the right wall and a staircase that went upstairs.

She looked to the stairs and quickly ruled them out. So far, the murders had taken places in alleys. It made her think the killer was drawing them out rather than taking the chance of venturing into the spaces where the women lived.

That could just be coincidence, she thought. *If he knows them well enough, maybe he'd be brave enough to knock on their door and go right in.*

She had to trust her instinct. It almost pained her to do so, but she dashed back out of the building and to the street. Alleys…that's what she needed to look for. That's where the killer had struck before and she didn't see why he'd change up his methods.

In the street, she nearly ran into a man of about fifty. He was scrawny and had a long, white beard that was stained with dirt. "Sir, please…I'm looking for a woman named Gina. Do you know anyone named Gina around here?"

The man looked frightened, probably at the urgency in her voice. He shook his head and wandered away from her, giving her an untrusting look. Again, Ava fought the urge to pull her badge and let him know she was with the police. If she and Frank had learned anything over the past few days, the fact that she was a member of the NYPD might hurt her more than help her in this part of town.

She ran past the next building and stopped at the next one, as an alleyway ran along between it and the neighboring building. She tried the door and found it locked. She knocked furiously on it and when no one answered, she pressed her ear to it to make sure there was no one simply hiding inside. Afterall, she *was* knocking pretty hard; she could very well be scaring the hell out of anyone on the other side.

As she listened, she did hear something on the other side. A soft sound, sort of a gurgling.

No…sort of *choking*.

With her heart leaping up into her chest, Ava drew her sidearm. Clutching it tightly in both hands, she took two steps back and then charged at the door with her shoulder lowered. She slammed into it, and it gave easily—so easily that she stumbled and fell to the floor. As she slid, her shoulder screaming and aching in fury, she got a very brief look at the place.

It was a basic one-room set-up, little temporary dividing walls set up between cots. From what she could see, the place was empty with the exception of a single man. This man was lying on his cot and sat up quickly, a snore caught in throat. The snore alone, even as he sprang awake, told Ava all she needed to know. She'd not heard choking from the other side of the door. She'd heard this man's snoring.

Jesus, Ava, she heard Clarence say in her head. *You need to calm down. You need to focus and get your head in this, or someone is going to die.*

"What in the blazes are…who are you?" the formerly sleeping man asked.

"Sorry, sir. I'm a detective and I—"

"A *woman* detective?" the man asked. He asked in a way that made her think the man was under the impression that he may still be asleep and having a very surreal dream.

As she got to her feet, making sure to hold her gun behind her as to not alarm the poor man, she withdrew her badge and showed it to him. "Yes, a woman detective. And I'm currently trying to prevent a murder. Sir...do you by any chance know a woman named Gina that lives around here? On this block or maybe one of the neighboring ones?"

Sleepily and still startled, the man nodded. "I know a Gina, yes. Sorry, but I'm, not sure of her last name. She brought me soup when I started with this God awful cold a few days ago and I—"

"Where, sir? Where does she live?"

He hitched a finger to the left, back toward the way Ava had come from. "Over that way. Two buildings down. In one of those so-called apartments."

The place I chose to ignore, she thought shamefully. "Do you know which room?"

"No, sorry. One on the first floor, though. There's an alley behind it that—"

"Thank you, sir!"

Ava got to her feet and ran through the doorway, realizing that she'd knocked it off of the hinges. In an almost comical way, she made a mental note to come back and fix it for him. This thought was obliterated by a bit of self-ridicule. *You skipped that entire building based on what you thought were facts. You tried to draw a conclusion from just two cases and look what it's done...*

She forced these thoughts out of her way as she came back to the fragile-looking apartment building. Sprinting back inside, she headed straight for the back. If there was indeed an alley back there as the sleeping man had said, maybe the killer *was* sticking to what he knew. If that was the case, maybe Gina's apartment was close to the back of the place.

She did the exact same thing she'd done back at the last building. She started at the last door to the right, placing her ear to the door. Right away, she heard something—a sliding sound, followed by a low mewling noise. Not quite a moan, but closer to a subdued shriek. A shriek that was being weakened and closed off.

For the second time in less than two minutes, Ava stepped back and prepared to knock a door down. Wanting to avoid the same stumbling mistake as before, she decided to use her legs this time. She delivered a well-placed kick right along the frame on the knob side of the door. The door went flying in, nearly popping entirely off of the frame. Just another indicator of how badly constructed these tenement buildings were.

Ava took everything in at once, processing every bit of information. The apartment consisted of one room. A cot sat against the far right wall. A glass jar of some sort of vegetable sat on the floor by the cot. A few sets of clothes hung on old hangers by the back door. The back door…it was open, revealing a filthy alley. Sunlight trickled in through the opened door, falling directly on the two bodies on the floor.

A man was perched on top of a woman. The woman was lying on her chest, the man pinning her down with a knee. He was pulling on something that was wrapped around the woman's neck, causing her to arch back in a painful U-shape.

The man turned around at the commotion made by Ava's sudden entrance. Seeing her and the gun, he released the scarf at once and bolted for the door. Ava found it a bit harder to pull the trigger than she'd expected. She waited perhaps a second too long, getting off the shot at the last moment as half of the man's body was already through the doorway.

The shot took him high in the hip, though. It sent him sprawling hard to the right, falling to the ground. Ava could not see where he hit the ground, as it was blocked by the wall. She ran for the other side of the apartment, to the opened door. She bent down just long enough to see if Gina was still alive. When she saw that she was coughing and hitching for breath, that was enough for her. She was more concerned about the killer getting away.

"I'll be right back," Ava said.

Gina nodded as Ava stepped quickly through the door.

Ava looked to the left, in the direction of where the man had fallen, and did not have quite enough time to register what she was seeing. The man was leaning against the wall and the moment she came through the doorway, he threw something at her. She did not realize this until the something hit her in the chest. It hurt like hell and knocked the wind out of her. She did not realize it was a brick until she was stumbling backward, and the brick clattered to the ground.

Rather than run away, the man charged at her, hitching up a bit of his left side where she'd shot him just above the waist. She halted this attack by bringing her right hand across. With the gun still in her grasp, the punch had more impact. He went falling hard to the right where he connected with the side of the building.

"Don't you dare move again, or I'll put another slug in you," Ava said. "Stay right there!"

Moaning in pain and effort, the man slid down the side of the wall. He seemed to have no fight left in him, the punch having effectively rung his bell. Ava held her gun on him, aiming it at his chest. Her cuffs were clasped to her belt and as she reached for them, she watched as the man—presumably Ted Johnson—started to blink his eyes rapidly, trying to clear the effects of her punch to his head.

Ava grabbed the cuffs and had them in her hand when Johnson moved. It was the second time he'd caught her by surprise and even as she felt yet another projectile hit her, she yelled at herself internally. *How the hell are you letting this happen?*

This time, the projectile was much less innocent than a thrown brick. In desperation, Johnson had grabbed a handful of dirt and grime from the ground and simply tossed it up into her face. Grit got into her eyes, and she stumbled back in surprise, as she tried blinking the filth away.

He was at her knees right away and she was falling before she knew it. When her back struck the ground, she felt her breath rushing out of her again. She did her best to bring her knee up, knowing that he was about to pounce on her, but he was already there. His left arm found her right arm and held it down so she could not shoot him again.

"I can kill you, too," he said. "Some kind of show-off cop, right? Just a woman. No one will care…no one will care…"

He pressed himself down on her in a way that made her think he might have sexual assault in mind, too. With his weight pressing down on her and his left hand clutching her left to the ground, he used his free hand to wrap around her neck. His grip was tight, his hand massive and strong.

Right away, she felt the pressure closing off her windpipe. She tried to fight against him but could only get her left leg up, and that was doing no good. She toyed with the idea of firing another shot and hoping it might attract the attention of someone else, but that might only put a passerby in danger.

With her breath running out and her vision growing hazy, she again scolded herself. *Frank should be with you. If he were here, this guy would be cuffed, and we'd already be on our way back to the station.*

Instead, here she was being strangled, maybe about twenty seconds from death. She gave one more final surge of anger and strength as she tried to fight him off, but he was not budging. He looked down at her with a calm sort of menace as she was nearly to the point of closing her eyes, not wanting his wretched face to be the last thing she saw before she died.

Her lungs were aching, demanding air, but she could not draw any in. She gripped her fingers around the gun, trying to will herself to use one more last surge of adrenaline, one last surge of strength. But there was nothing. Her oxygen-starved body was too desperate to do much of anything and—

Oddly, it seemed to start to rain out of nowhere. This was accompanied by an odd noise, something that sounded both very close and very far away at the same time. Whatever it was, Johnson must have noticed it, too. His eyes went wide, then narrow. His grip around her neck eased and he slowly fell off of her.

She made a weak grunt as she sucked in air and pushed him off of her. As she scrambled back a bit, not yet strong enough to get to her feet, she saw what had happened.

Gina was in front of her, kneeling on the ground. She held what looked like a small shard of glass in her hand. No, not a shard—the bottom to a jar. Distantly, Ava recalled seeing the jar of some sort of vegetable inside the apartment. The rain Ava had felt had likely been the juices from inside of it spilling down on her as Gina smashed the jar against the side of Johnson's head. As Ava's senses became more and more present, she also realized that there were great many beans on the ground around her.

"Thank you," Ava said in a thin, raspy voice. She was beyond embarrassed, but also grateful to be alive. Another ten seconds under Johnson's grip and she would probably have died.

Damn. Johnson…

She staggered to her feet and looked down at the murderer. He was still very much alive but was stationary on the ground. He lay on his back, bleeding from his head and the gunshot to his waist. He was opening his mouth, trying to say something, but nothing came out.

"You okay?" Gina asked.

"Yeah. You?"

Gina nodded as she looked to the handcuffs Ava had dropped on the ground. Ava scooped them up, alarmed at just how off balance she still felt. When she hobbled over to Johnson and pushed him over on his side to cuff him, he did not fight. She lipped the cuffs on and locked them in place.

He never complained through the process. If anything, he seemed distracted. As she moved him around, she noticed his eyes flickering in the direction of Gina's back door. She wasn't too sure, but Ava thought he was staring at the scarf he had dropped, eyeing it as if there was some answer there that might help him make sense of all he'd done.

CHAPTER THIRTY THREE

Ava was sitting on the edge of the doctor's examination table when the door opened. She'd already been seen by the doctor, and he'd let her know that her partner was out in the waiting area. So when Frank stepped in, it wasn't a surprise—but it was certainly a welcome sight. When Frank came in, he looked both relieved and irritated. Given their partnership thus far, it was a mix of emotions that she was coming to know far too well.

"I'm mad at you," he said as he closed the door behind him.

"I figured. I know I should have come to get you, but…I knew what was waiting for me at the precinct after everything that went down with Duggar."

"I get that. But going off after a killer by yourself…"

"I didn't know how much time I had. And now that I know how everything played out, I also know that if I'd come back to the station to get you, we'd have a third dead body on our hands."

Frank nodded, stepping close to her. He took her hands in his and looked her in the eyes. "You're okay? The doc says so, but what do *you* say?"

"Well, I won't be singing anytime soon, that's for sure. My throat hurts. Hurts pretty bad, actually. But the doctor said he can't see any real damage."

"You're lucky, if you ask me. There's a whole mess of beans back at the crime scene to back that up."

"Yeah. She…well, she saved my life."

"That she did. Ah, but there's more proof that you may be the luckiest officer ever to grace my presence. Turns out, Duggar was selling information to some folks in the mob. He was not only looking for papers, but for kids. He'd come across illegals that were under sixteen and then inform the mob. The mob was then picking those kids up and using them to run some pretty dirty errands. We have no hard proof just yet, but we think there might have been some prostitution involved with the girls."

"My God."

"In other words, your hunch about Duggar uncovered all of this. Minard had been suspicious for a while but having him held for suspicion of murder got some people talking. So not only did he get charged, but there are some on the force that are now thankful you did what you did. Otherwise, no one would have ever found out what Duggar was really up to.”

This actually meant a great deal to Ava, but she held some of it back. “I’d consider that a win, then.”

“Ava…you could have died today. You get that, right?”

“Yes.”

“You have to be more careful. You have a son that cares about you. And a partner that cares about you, too.”

“I know,” she said, meeting his eyes.

She felt it again, that pull towards him. It was the same pull she’d felt out in the hallway of her apartment building several nights ago. Only this time, she did not intend to stop it. And as Frank slowly started to lean forward, it was apparent that he wasn’t going to stop it, either.

When their lips met, it felt surprisingly natural. With their hands still clasped, she felt him squeezing. She allowed herself to get lost in the moment, and the kiss did not end until the doctor came back into the room and did his best to ignore both of the red-faced, embarrassed detectives in his examination room.

***

She only took the full two days off of work because Minard had insisted on it. After the first day her throat had been feeling much better, though it did hurt to swallow a bit. When she finally came back to work, there was bruising around her throat and the embarrassment of knowing that a woman with a jar of beans had saved her life. But she also noticed that she wasn’t getting as many sideways glances or aggravated expressions as she made her way through the lobby and towards the bullpen.

As she headed for Frank’s desk, she realized that she was quite nervous. She’d spent the last two days at home with Jeffrey and her father, thinking something over. The kiss with Frank had proven to her that she trusted him beyond measure They’d kissed here and there since the first dizzying one at the doctor’s office and each time, it felt more and more natural.

She was pretty sure he felt the same and that was why she’d come to a certain decision. It made sense and she knew it was the right thing to do, but her stomach was in knots as she approached his desk on that Thursday morning.

When she came to his desk, she saw that he already had a chair waiting for her. She smiled at the gesture; she wouldn't have to sit on the edge of his desk anymore. As they locked eyes, she noticed a bit of commotion out on the bullpen floor. There were some whispered voices and someone uttering a curse as they looked at the newspaper. She wondered what sort of stories she'd missed while she'd been out. Maybe she had some catching up to do.

"Welcome back," Frank said.

"Thanks."

"Now that we're…well, *closer* now, do you think you'll be able to keep your mouth off of mine while we're at work."

"Oh, I'll do my very best," she said with a sly grin. The grin faded as the nerves took over. She knew that if she did not mention this now, she likely never would. She looked to his desk, to her hands, to the floor—everywhere but at him. As she avoided it for as long as she could, she noticed more frantic conversations out in the bullpen.

"Something wrong?" Frank asked.

"You're right. We are closer now," she said very quickly. "And because of that, I need to be honest with you."

"Okay. About what?"

She went ahead and blurted it out. She knew there was a chance he might think differently of her, but it felt good all the same. With each word she spoke, she felt a slight weight come off of her shoulders.

"I've been trying to solve Clarence's murder ever since I started working here. I've been doing it in secret and staking out people and places after hours every now and then."

"Okay," he said, tilting his head slightly. "I think that's only natural…though I'm not a fan of you traipsing around questionable parts of town at night."

"It's paid off," she said. "I have a name and a record of crimes to go with the name."

Frank leaned in closer. "Who is it?"

"A guy named Jim Spurlock."

Frank grimaced and sat back in his chair.

"You know the name?"

"Yeah. And though I don't think he's actually *in* the mob, he's got close friends that are. Ava…you need to be careful with this."

"I know. That's why I've come to you. I want you to help."

He said nothing for a while, but she could tell from his posture and the way he looked at her that he'd already made his decision. "How sure are you?"

"Pretty sure. I can walk you through the records, the timeline, the connection to Spurlock with other people, all of it."

"I don't doubt that," he said. "What I mean is are you sure it's something you want to pursue? Because for something like this, you need to be honest with yourself: Are you more interested in arresting this guy or do you want blood?"

"Both. He…he killed Clarence."

"You understand this couldn't be an on the books thing, right? It has to be kept in secret and even then, we—"

"Never mind. It's fine. I'll keep running it myself and—"

"No, I'll help. I just want you to be fully aware of what you're up against."

The anger that rose up in her was unexpected and it almost took her by complete surprise. She'd finally come clean with someone about this, and this was *not* how she'd expected it to go. Especially not from Frank.

"I said it's fine! I shouldn't have asked you to get involved."

"Ava, I need—"

But he was interrupted by the clamoring conversation that continued to grow behind them. They both turned and saw several officers walking quickly to the front doors, Captain Minard among them.

"What's going on?" Frank muttered as he got out of his seat.

Ava followed him into the small crowd of officers that were heading to the front of the building. She was next to Frank when he asked Officer Simmons: "What the hell is all this about?"

"Two suicides," Simmons said. "From what I hear, some man just shot himself in the head right in front of a bank just a few blocks from here."

"What?"

Someone opened the front doors, and they were all met with the sounds of commotion. People were talking loudly; the noise of motors were filling the street. Something with a siren went blazing by, likely a fire truck or ambulance.

"I don't understand…," Ava said.

Ahead of her, Minard made his way to the doors, and she got her answer. "It's the banks," he said, turning to everyone. "The stock market…it crashed overnight. We've got two suicides; one man jumped from the roof of his penthouse, and another shot himself in the head in front of a bank. All of the banks are closing for the day and people are getting antsy. No banks, no money…"

He left it at that as several officer stepped outside onto the street. Ava and Frank were among them, stepping out into streets that Ava had never seen quite so chaotic. On the corner on the other side of the street, three men were in a shouting match. A bit further down and to the right, a small mob of people were gathering in front of a bank and screaming.

Another siren went blazing by. This time Ava saw that it was indeed an ambulance. A man crossing the street was nearly struck by it.

"This is crazy," Frank said. "All because the banks…the stock market."

But even he couldn't finish it, and Ava thought she knew why. Because as much as they all wanted to pretend that they weren't' so dependent on money and the systems that managed its worth and doled it out, finances did indeed hold sway over their lives.

And when that was disrupted, everything else was, too.

Everything else came apart.

Slowly, Ava reached out and took Frank's hand. It went unspoken between them but as Ava looked out into the madness in the streets, she could not help but think that after this morning, the city—and maybe the entire nation beyond them—would never quite be the same.

NOW AVAILABLE!

CITY OF DEATH
An Ava Gold Mystery (Book 5)

1920s. New York City. When a wealthy white man is killed in Harlem, racial tensions flare throughout the city. Ava must delve into her old life in the jazz clubs and speakeasies of New York, fighting against a ticking clock before the entire city, on edge, explodes into racial riots.

"A MASTERPIECE OF THRILLER AND MYSTERY. Blake Pierce did a magnificent job developing characters with a psychological side so well described that we feel inside their minds, follow their fears and cheer for their success. Full of twists, this book will keep you awake until the turn of the last page."
--Books and Movie Reviews, Roberto Mattos (re Once Gone)

CITY OF DEATH (An Ava Gold Mystery—Book 5) is a new novel in a long-anticipated new series by #1 bestseller and USA Today bestselling author Blake Pierce, whose bestseller Once Gone (a free download) has received over 1,000 five star reviews.

In the rough streets of 1920s New York City, 34 year-old Ava Gold, a widower and single mom, claws her way up to become the first female homicide detective in her NYPD precinct. She is as tough as they come, and willing to hold her own in a man's world.

When a black musician is accused of murdering a wealthy white Manhattanite, Ava senses all is not what it seems. Determined to track down the real killer, Ava dives back into her old life: the Harlem world of clubs. But her time is short, and there is only one thing she can be sure of: this killer will strike again.

A heart-pounding suspense thriller filled with shocking twists, the authentic and atmospheric AVA GOLD MYSTERY SERIES is a riveting page-turner, endearing us to a strong and brilliant character that will capture your heart and keep you reading late into the night.

Book #6 in the series—CITY OF VICE—is now also available.

Blake Pierce

Blake Pierce is the USA Today bestselling author of the RILEY PAGE mystery series, which includes seventeen books. Blake Pierce is also the author of the MACKENZIE WHITE mystery series, comprising fourteen books; of the AVERY BLACK mystery series, comprising six books; of the KERI LOCKE mystery series, comprising five books; of the MAKING OF RILEY PAIGE mystery series, comprising six books; of the KATE WISE mystery series, comprising seven books; of the CHLOE FINE psychological suspense mystery, comprising six books; of the JESSE HUNT psychological suspense thriller series, comprising twenty one books; of the AU PAIR psychological suspense thriller series, comprising three books; of the ZOE PRIME mystery series, comprising six books; of the ADELE SHARP mystery series, comprising fifteen books, of the EUROPEAN VOYAGE cozy mystery series, comprising four books; of the new LAURA FROST FBI suspense thriller, comprising six books (and counting); of the new ELLA DARK FBI suspense thriller, comprising eleven books (and counting); of the A YEAR IN EUROPE cozy mystery series, comprising nine books, of the AVA GOLD mystery series, comprising six books (and counting); and of the RACHEL GIFT mystery series, comprising six books (and counting).

An avid reader and lifelong fan of the mystery and thriller genres, Blake loves to hear from you, so please feel free to visit www.blakepierceauthor.com to learn more and stay in touch.

BOOKS BY BLAKE PIERCE

RACHEL GIFT MYSTERY SERIES
HER LAST WISH (Book #1)
HER LAST CHANCE (Book #2)
HER LAST HOPE (Book #3)
HER LAST FEAR (Book #4)
HER LAST CHOICE (Book #5)
HER LAST BREATH (Book #6)

AVA GOLD MYSTERY SERIES
CITY OF PREY (Book #1)
CITY OF FEAR (Book #2)
CITY OF BONES (Book #3)
CITY OF GHOSTS (Book #4)
CITY OF DEATH (Book #5)
CITY OF VICE (Book #6)

A YEAR IN EUROPE
A MURDER IN PARIS (Book #1)
DEATH IN FLORENCE (Book #2)
VENGEANCE IN VIENNA (Book #3)
A FATALITY IN SPAIN (Book #4)

ELLA DARK FBI SUSPENSE THRILLER
GIRL, ALONE (Book #1)
GIRL, TAKEN (Book #2)
GIRL, HUNTED (Book #3)
GIRL, SILENCED (Book #4)
GIRL, VANISHED (Book 5)
GIRL ERASED (Book #6)
GIRL, FORSAKEN (Book #7)
GIRL, TRAPPED (Book #8)
GIRL, EXPENDABLE (Book #9)
GIRL, ESCAPED (Book #10)
GIRL, HIS (Book #11)

LAURA FROST FBI SUSPENSE THRILLER
ALREADY GONE (Book #1)
ALREADY SEEN (Book #2)
ALREADY TRAPPED (Book #3)
ALREADY MISSING (Book #4)
ALREADY DEAD (Book #5)
ALREADY TAKEN (Book #6)

EUROPEAN VOYAGE COZY MYSTERY SERIES
MURDER (AND BAKLAVA) (Book #1)
DEATH (AND APPLE STRUDEL) (Book #2)
CRIME (AND LAGER) (Book #3)
MISFORTUNE (AND GOUDA) (Book #4)
CALAMITY (AND A DANISH) (Book #5)
MAYHEM (AND HERRING) (Book #6)

ADELE SHARP MYSTERY SERIES
LEFT TO DIE (Book #1)
LEFT TO RUN (Book #2)
LEFT TO HIDE (Book #3)
LEFT TO KILL (Book #4)
LEFT TO MURDER (Book #5)
LEFT TO ENVY (Book #6)
LEFT TO LAPSE (Book #7)
LEFT TO VANISH (Book #8)
LEFT TO HUNT (Book #9)
LEFT TO FEAR (Book #10)
LEFT TO PREY (Book #11)
LEFT TO LURE (Book #12)
LEFT TO CRAVE (Book #13)
LEFT TO LOATHE (Book #14)
LEFT TO HARM (Book #15)

THE AU PAIR SERIES
ALMOST GONE (Book#1)
ALMOST LOST (Book #2)
ALMOST DEAD (Book #3)

ZOE PRIME MYSTERY SERIES
FACE OF DEATH (Book#1)

FACE OF MURDER (Book #2)
FACE OF FEAR (Book #3)
FACE OF MADNESS (Book #4)
FACE OF FURY (Book #5)
FACE OF DARKNESS (Book #6)

A JESSIE HUNT PSYCHOLOGICAL SUSPENSE SERIES
THE PERFECT WIFE (Book #1)
THE PERFECT BLOCK (Book #2)
THE PERFECT HOUSE (Book #3)
THE PERFECT SMILE (Book #4)
THE PERFECT LIE (Book #5)
THE PERFECT LOOK (Book #6)
THE PERFECT AFFAIR (Book #7)
THE PERFECT ALIBI (Book #8)
THE PERFECT NEIGHBOR (Book #9)
THE PERFECT DISGUISE (Book #10)
THE PERFECT SECRET (Book #11)
THE PERFECT FAÇADE (Book #12)
THE PERFECT IMPRESSION (Book #13)
THE PERFECT DECEIT (Book #14)
THE PERFECT MISTRESS (Book #15)
THE PERFECT IMAGE (Book #16)
THE PERFECT VEIL (Book #17)
THE PERFECT INDISCRETION (Book #18)
THE PERFECT RUMOR (Book #19)
THE PERFECT COUPLE (Book #20)
THE PERFECT MURDER (Book #21)

CHLOE FINE PSYCHOLOGICAL SUSPENSE SERIES
NEXT DOOR (Book #1)
A NEIGHBOR'S LIE (Book #2)
CUL DE SAC (Book #3)
SILENT NEIGHBOR (Book #4)
HOMECOMING (Book #5)
TINTED WINDOWS (Book #6)

KATE WISE MYSTERY SERIES
IF SHE KNEW (Book #1)
IF SHE SAW (Book #2)

BEFORE HE SINS (Book #7)
BEFORE HE HUNTS (Book #8)
BEFORE HE PREYS (Book #9)
BEFORE HE LONGS (Book #10)
BEFORE HE LAPSES (Book #11)
BEFORE HE ENVIES (Book #12)
BEFORE HE STALKS (Book #13)
BEFORE HE HARMS (Book #14)

AVERY BLACK MYSTERY SERIES
CAUSE TO KILL (Book #1)
CAUSE TO RUN (Book #2)
CAUSE TO HIDE (Book #3)
CAUSE TO FEAR (Book #4)
CAUSE TO SAVE (Book #5)
CAUSE TO DREAD (Book #6)

KERI LOCKE MYSTERY SERIES
A TRACE OF DEATH (Book #1)
A TRACE OF MURDER (Book #2)
A TRACE OF VICE (Book #3)
A TRACE OF CRIME (Book #4)
A TRACE OF HOPE (Book #5)

www.ingramcontent.com/pod-product-compliance
Lightning Source LLC
Chambersburg PA
CBHW021700110726

47902CB00007B/2009